ONE

Club whore. Not my favorite title, but one ...   n more than the immediate connotations most people connected with it. It wasn't something I aspired to be as a little girl dreaming of a bright future, but that future dimmed when life delivered me too many of the ugly truths of the universe in too few years.

I'm not going to sit and whine about a happy childhood that was shattered and turned into a nightmare after one horrible night, nor am I going to recount the year I spent dancing on a pole to put food on the table and a roof over my head. That ain't me. I'm a survivor. I'll take what life throws at me and figure out a way to catch it with a smile. I find solace in worlds of fantasy and magic, places where I can escape the darkness and evil of the real world. I laugh as much as I can, try not to take life too seriously. Otherwise, I'd never get out alive. No matter what, I'm not letting the bitterness of this world settle in and taint my soul. I did what I could to claw my way out of a life that threatened to ruin me, to find one that suited me, where I fit, where I had a family.

"Macy!" Jagger yelled at me.

I whirled around on my barstool. I'd been alone at the bar, enjoying an unusual moment of silence. I was never silent. And around here, I was hardly ever stationary.

"Yeah, hon?" I replied with a small grin.

"Get me a beer, and get your sweet ass over here," he commanded from his spot at a table where he was flanked by Charley and Levi.

I rolled my eyes and bent over to snag a beer from the fridge.

"I got it, kiddo," I reassured the Prospect, who had rushed to help me.

I gave him a wink. They got enough shit from the boys, I didn't mind doing what I could to make their lives easier.

I sauntered up to the table, my eyes on Jagger. I stopped just out of his reach and dangled the beer from my hand.

"Anyone ever teach you a word that, in polite society, comes after a request? Rhymes with cheese?" I asked with a sickly sweet tone.

Jagger shook his head and Levi chuckled.

"Beautiful and intelligent, Macy. Won't you please hand me that chilled beverage and sit that tight behind on my knee?" his gravelly voice requested.

He didn't wait for me to move, just leaned out of his chair and tagged my waist, yanking me onto his lap. I let out a small squeal but laughed.

He nuzzled my neck affectionately and I leaned into his hold.

I liked Jagger. Had a soft spot for him. He wasn't what

OUTSIDE THE LINES

A SONS OF TEMPLAR NOVELLA

ANNE MALCOLM

most women would call handsome, given the fact he had a scar that marred half of his face, from his temple to the side of his nose, it was jagged, angry and puckered. His jaw was sharp and masculine, although it was covered by a long beard. His hair was unruly and inky black, but always shiny and clean. He wasn't tall—he was taller than me, even in heels, but that wasn't saying much—but he was stocky and packed with muscle. It was his eyes that captured me the most. They were the most vibrant green I'd ever encountered, like two emeralds shining from his head. He also had the most gifted tongue I'd ever experienced. Plus, he treated me with respect. Most of the boys did, but he treated me like a friend as well as a bed mate, and we'd spend hours talking after he'd used that gifted tongue along with other appendages.

"You looked mighty deep in thought over there darlin'," he commented giving me a squeeze. "Anything me and my most knowledgeable advisors can help with?" He nodded to Charley and Levi, who did their best to look wise.

I gave them a look, then burst out laughing.

Charley was little more than a kid, he'd prospected straight out of high school and earned his patch before he could even legally drink. He was still only twenty and his boyish looks were yet to be corrupted and hardened by the life he'd chosen to lead. His close-cropped blond hair and classically handsome face made him easily mistaken for a college kid. Though, you only needed to get a look at his patch and the tattoos already serving as a patchwork over his muscled body to learn the truth. He even had SONS tattooed on his knuckles, in addition to the tattoo spanning his back. The MC was his life. He'd leave it only in a coffin—or handcuffs.

Levi was one of the older members, he'd been with the

New Mexico chapter of The Sons of Templar for as many years as I'd been alive. His shaggy graying hair brushed his shoulders and he was clinging to his Chopper style mustache, despite it leaving the right side of trendy decades prior. His tattoos were faded and his belly protruding from too much beer, but he was still someone you'd be pretty stupid to get on the wrong side of, especially since you never saw him without a big scary knife strapped to his belt.

"Nothing that I want to trouble you three with," I said taking a pull of my beer. "I'll leave you to solving things like world hunger and global warming," I teased fondly.

Though they were hardened men, who I knew could be scary as shit did the occasion arise, they were also my family. Loyal to a fault, they would die for each other. I'd been with them for two years and felt like maybe they'd stick their necks out for me too. Or maybe that was my darned optimism shining through.

After laughing and shooting the shit with the men, more members arrived and the start of the weekly Friday night party began. Not that these men needed a designated night to get loose.

More club girls, namely Scarlett and Kimberly took it upon themselves to get up on the pole in the corner of the room and do a strip show for the boys at one point, not that they had much covering themselves to begin with. Here, there were two kinds of club girls. Scar and Kim, who were all about the shortest skirts, the highest heels, and the most skin. They weren't fazed about having relations in public. Evidenced by the fact, Scar just let one of the guys yank her off the stage and drag her into a dimly lit, but still visible corner to do the nasty. Then there were girls like me. Sure I liked my heels, but my clothing erred on the hippy side. I was less than likely to be found sprawled across the hood of a car and photographed for a men's magazine editorial. And, I was not into public sex. Luckily, the men respected this, and never tried to go past heavy petting at these things.

"How about we blow this joint?" Jagger murmured in my ear, his hand tickling the edge of my skirt.

I smiled and nodded slightly, my eyes catching on something across the room. More like someone. Hansen's eyes burned into me and did not leave mine even as Jagger led me away by the hand. I struggled against the feeling I got in that moment, it was the same feeling I'd had whenever those blue eyes caught mine. I also struggled with the obvious fury dancing behind those eyes as he focused on Jagger's hand in mine. Then the fury was gone, replaced by a blank stare, one that flickered away from me just before I rounded the corner.

―――――――

"SURE YOU DON'T WANNA talk about whatever had you a million miles away?" Jagger asked, puffing on his smoke.

I moved my head to look at his profile. "Nothing to trouble your pretty little head about," I teased softly.

Jagger moved his own head, regarding me.

We'd just finished round two of a very productive sexathon. I was exhausted and definitely sated. Like always, I felt happy to chill in his room and just hang.

"Your grandma?" he guessed, not letting it go.

I snorted. "I try not to waste too much cranial power on that old bat. I already commit an hour a week to being in her presence, that's enough," I told him honestly.

Apart from the club, my grandma was the only shred of family I had on this earth. She was mean as they came, and wasting away in an old folks' home after being diagnosed with Alzheimer's. Not that she'd lost her marbles. She had a firm enough grip on those things to remember what a disappointment I was and made sure to remind me of that every time she saw me. Jagger was the only one who knew about her, about how deep her sharp tongue cut me.

"You know..." Jagger said slowly taking a drag of his smoke, his expression turning serious, "...you're better than this." He waved his hand around the room. "Not that I don't love your company, inside and outside the bedroom..." he winked before his face turned serious again, "...but this life, you can do better. You deserve better. You're smart, beautiful. World's got more to offer you than this."

I jerked slightly at such a speech coming from Jagger. He lived for the club. Breathed it. He'd been here way longer than my two years, considering he was in his early thirties and had patched in when he was younger than me. I went up on my elbow and rested my head in my hand.

"Yeah, right, I've got so much to offer the world," I replied sarcastically. "Plus, you'd be lost without me. Admit it," I teased.

Jagger's face failed to lighten at my words. "Serious, babe. There's some people who suit the life, who deserve to live in the gray. You deserve more, more than a bunch of bikers can give you," he told me.

I let his words sink in. "You're wrong," I whispered. "I've seen what the world's like outside this... without a family... without anyone. It's not pretty. And it sure as shit doesn't have anything to offer me," I replied decisively. Again, my voice didn't hold self-pity, only confidence. Confidence that this was the best life for me. For now anyway. I wasn't too crash hot on making future plans. I was a *live in the now* type of girl.

He gave me a searching look, then a smile came back to his face. He stubbed out his smoke and tagged my hips, dragging me on top of him.

"Well, I sure as shit have something to offer you," he murmured. His hard-on pressing into my stomach serving as evidence.

I let the little tingle of desire warm up my entire body, and for the next half an hour, let that be the only thing I thought of.

I CLOSED the door to Jagger's room quietly. It was the early hours of the morning, the only time the clubhouse was as silent as a tomb. It was my favorite time. When I could trail my fingers along the mismatched frames in the hallway, looking at the history of the brotherhood, of the loyalty keeping this family together. Yes, the underbelly of such a family may be gritty and slide right into the black side of black and white, but at least they didn't lie about who they were. Most families buried their secrets and wrongdoings in closets, behind the family photos and kid's toys. They were slaves to a society that told you the right way to live, the right way to act, and chained you to that life. The life that I'd rather die than commit myself to. I knew, if I were a man, I would have patched into the Sons. But I wasn't. My vagina gave me two options, if I wanted to be part of the life that seemed to fit me perfectly, it was club girl or Old Lady.

Going into the club, I didn't know anything about it. I was

just a girl who didn't know who she was, looking for somewhere to fit in. I discovered the way the Sons lived, found out I liked it, and just kind of slipped into the role of being someone who didn't belong to anyone in particular—just the club in general. I wanted to be an Old Lady. Not in the way Kim and Scar desperately wanted to sink their claws into someone, for power, money, or the thrill of being hooked to an 'outlaw.' No. I wanted the unconditional, unfathomable dedication and love that that title represented. A man who was devoted to me, brothers who treated me with the respect that old ladies got. I wanted a permanent place in the family. It hadn't worked out that way, I didn't know if it ever would. I knew that 'club whore' had a time limit. A ticking clock if you will.

I had made it to the common room, where various club members were passed out. Some had half-naked women draped over them, others were clutching half full bottles of spirits. I shook my head at Levi, who was snoring on the pool table with two girls tucked under each arm.

Walking to the kitchen, my aim was to get a glass of water and a snack before I headed home to score approximately four hours of shut eye. Then I would chain myself to my computer and go to work on my design projects. That plan was changed when I saw the kitchen was in a state of disarray, to put it mildly. Someone had obviously decided to have a drunken cook up then forgotten to commence the drunken clean up. I sighed and shook my head.

"Worse than teenagers," I muttered to myself.

Setting my bag on the counter, I unearthed my phone and headphones. Music was one of the many things I indulged in that helped me escape. Helped me remind myself to live and be happy, regardless of my past. So, a half hour later, that's what I was doing, dancing and singing along to my favorite song while cleaning up the mess. I didn't mind really. It was expected that I do shit like this. It may have been on the wrong side of sexist, and sometimes it did grate me, but most of the time I did it with no complaints. They were family. What they gave me in return was worth washing a few dirty dishes. I was swirling around, lost in the music readying myself to do a final wipe down then leave.

Then my eyes met something I didn't expect.

A figure stood in the doorway. I covered my mouth to muffle the scream that came with my fright. My heart didn't stop beating when I realized it was familiar eyes that burned into mine.

My face burned red with embarrassment. Hansen, the man who pretty much consumed my mind, the man who I fantasized about but never paid any attention to me stood right in the door. Right now, though, his eyes didn't hold the look of a man who barely gave me a second glance for the past year. No. They held hunger. Heat.

I'd been so busy inspecting this hunger, shocked by the desire in his gaze, my music was still playing in my ears. I yanked one of my earphones out, preparing myself to say—I had no idea what. Hansen pushed off the doorway and closed the distance between us. His hands clutched the sides of my neck and his mouth dipped onto mine, silencing whatever no doubt stupid thing I was going to say.

I was so shocked I didn't respond at first. Then his tongue probed mine, kissing me with ferocity, an intensity that I'd never even known existed. My whole body sank into his and I gave into the kiss, making a little sound at the back of my throat as his touch sent pinpricks of arousal up and down my spine. His hands moved to my ass and he lifted me, setting me down on the counter, so his crotch pressed into mine. I wrapped my legs around him, needing him closer. It felt like I'd never had sex before, I was that desperate. It was like I hadn't been thoroughly satisfied a few hours ago. Well, I thought I'd been satisfied. This kiss, the promise behind it, showed me I didn't know what satisfaction was.

Abruptly, Hansen's mouth disengaged from mine, his eyes hardening as he seemed to catch himself. He stared at me a long moment, fury replacing the hot desire that had been there moments before. He stepped back quickly, causing me to lose my purchase on his delightful body.

I also lost the ability to speak as his angry stare silenced me. His eyes quickly ran over my body then he turned on his heel and left.

Without a word.

Man just kissed the living shit out of me and *left?*

What. The. Fuck.

I sat on the counter shocked, still half deafened by the music in my ears.

"Did that really happen?" I asked the empty room.

The room, of course, had no answer.

OVER THE NEXT WEEK, Hansen avoided me like I had some kind of flesh eating virus. Every time I entered the clubhouse, his eyes turned dark and his face turned tight, it seemed he did everything in his power to make sure I didn't come within five feet of him.

That hurt.

No, that *killed*.

I didn't think I was a bad kisser. Apparently so. I'd let myself hope that *that* kiss meant he finally *saw* me and recognized the attraction. That, and the fact that I'd been pining after him since the moment he arrived from the Nevada chapter. Just waiting for him to notice me, hoping that he'd see beyond the label I'd stuck myself with, and maybe consider me as something more. That hope went down in flames with the burn of cold indifference.

It didn't help the guys had seemed to decide to treat me like some kind of leper also. They joked with me, were easily affectionate, like always, but nothing over G rated. No one got frisky, no one yanked me off into their rooms, no one even suggested it. It confused me. Hurt me. Was I getting phased out? Were they sick of me? Was my adopted family abandoning me?

"You got the clap or something?" a throaty voice asked from beside me.

I moved my eyes from the perusal of my beer bottle to Scarlett, who had seated herself behind me on the sofa. Her blonde hair was piled atop her head, her face slathered with expertly applied, yet completely over the top makeup. It wasn't bitchy, the expression on that made up face was merely curious.

"Excuse me?" I asked, confused.

"The clap? Herpes, warts? Something to make the boys put you in quarantine for?" she clarified.

I jerked back. I was religious about protection. I knew my sexual habits weren't what mainstream society deemed as appropriate for a woman, I didn't give a shit. I certainly wasn't going to feed the stereotype that club girls were somehow *dirty*.

"No, of course not," I exclaimed hotly.

She shrugged her shoulders, leaning back on the sofa. "Well, something's got them..." she nodded at a couple of the men who were sitting at the bar, "...making sure Kim and I are kept busy the past week. Not that I'm complaining, but whatever that something is, seems to have gotten you on the no screw list," she observed with a raised brow. I expected there to be some kind of bitchy satisfaction at this, but there was only curiosity and if I wasn't imagining it, concern.

I bit my lip. My stomach swirled at the thought of losing this. The only place where I felt I belonged. Then something struck me. A week. A week exactly since Hansen had kissed me senseless in the kitchen. A week since I'd developed a third eye or some other disfigurement only visible to bikers.

I stood, my worry turning to anger quickly.

"Thanks, I owe you one," I told Scarlett.

She looked at me like I was slightly crazy, but most people did that around here, thanks to the fact my mouth always seemed to outrun my mind.

"Sure, no problem," she replied as I turned my well-heeled toes toward the bar. The bar where Hansen was sitting with his back to me.

Charley watched me approach with wide eyes, his glance moving toward where my own were narrowed.

"Oh shit," he muttered under his breath.

I ignored that and moved to stand beside Hansen getting right in his face.

"You and me need to have a chat, *now*," I demanded sharply.

He didn't look at me. "Got nothing to say to you," his voice was cold.

I masked the pain at his tone, at his dismissal. "Isn't that mighty convenient. You don't have to say anything, considering I'm the one that's gonna be speaking," I snapped.

I didn't wait for another no doubt biting response, I grabbed his muscled arm and yanked. I was under no illusions about my strength or lack of it. I was short, even in my wedged boots, and despite the fact I considered Cheetos, a food group, I weighed a lot less than Hansen.

Still, he let me drag him off and around the corner, out of sight of the peanut gallery. He jerked his arm out of my grasp when we'd moved into the deserted hallway.

He stepped forward, and without meaning to, I retreated so my back hit the wall.

"You don't ever..." he spoke quietly, his body taut, "...speak to me like that in front of my brothers again."

I shivered at that blankness that settled over his face. This wasn't him. He might have silenced me with biting stares over the past week, but before that he was anything but cold. He didn't sleep with any of the girls here, that didn't mean he didn't show them respect. He laughed easily with the men, and although he never laughed in my direction or at one of my jokes, it was still easy to see he didn't take himself or his general badassness too seriously.

And he was a badass. Down to his hulking frame, one that towered over me with rippling muscles that had him looking like some kind of fitness model. His bald head accentuated his sharp and defined features, only enhancing his hotness. Which was weird, considering I always thought I'd liked men with shaggy hair—apparently not.

I didn't let myself turn into a squeaking female at his tone. "How about you don't go around kissing me, ignoring me, and then turning me into a leper. Then I won't have to talk to you like that to get your attention, since all other attempts have been met with a badass biker '*don't mess with me stare,*'" I snapped back.

I didn't know where this anger was coming from. I wasn't an angry person. Actively, I shied away from confrontation, didn't need it in my life. Right now it seemed I was ready to spit tacks.

Hansen's entire body stilled.

"You want to tell me what was so bad about my kissing skills for you to give me the cold shoulder for the past week? And then have every guy in here treat me like their little sister, instead of what I am?" I continued.

Shit. *Did I just say kissing skills?*

Hansen stared at me, searching my face. "What you are?" he repeated.

I observed the fact his features hardened exponentially as he uttered this.

"Yes. What I am. What I've been for the past two years," I snapped.

He didn't reply, his jaw tightening.

I made a decision. Whatever was going on here was not one sided. Even now, I felt the heat sizzle between us. If I wanted happiness, wanted him, I had to take it. Or at least, try. I stepped forward, clutching the sides of his cut lightly.

"I'm not the only one feeling this," I murmured, my voice shaking. "I know you feel it too."

Hansen seemed to consider my words for a moment,

appearing like he was inspecting the attraction between us. Then he clutched my wrists and shoved them away roughly.

"I don't," he clipped coldly. "Kissing you was a mistake. One I won't make again," he promised, then didn't waste any time in turning his back on me.

I sagged against the wall, trying not to admit my heart was in little pieces at that moment. That I hadn't been humiliated and rejected by the man who I'd been crushing on for the better part of a year. I'd failed on that score.

TWO

I didn't get much time to wallow in self-pity at Hansen's cold rejection. Not when the boys from the Cali chapter thundered in with a wave of testosterone and proved that it was possible for a sexy glare to melt panties. They caused the club to go into full badass mode as the set about rescuing Brock's—sexy surfer biker hybrid who changed my stance on thinking man buns were stupid—Old Lady from some guy who had kidnapped her. Yes, *kidnapped* her. I'd been with the club for a while, and we may have had some dramas, but we'd never had a kidnapping.

It was all hands on deck, and I was so busy helping out with shit I didn't notice the fact the boys were yet to touch me, despite Hansen's rejection. I was further distracted when a beautiful redhead with some seriously gnarly wounds was brought in. It was my task to hang out with her while she was bedridden and her old man did whatever club shit us females were not allowed to know about. Not that it was a chore. She was awesome, even battling blood loss and recovering from a kidnapping she was a freaking knockout.

It hurt my heart just a little to see how dedicated, how in love, Brock was with her. His eyes touched her when she wasn't looking, and he looked at her like she was the only thing tethering him to this earth. His reason for breathing. Even Bull's—a seriously scary biker who looked like he had the ability to kill someone with a biting glance—eyes seemed to soften when she smiled at him. She had the love of not only a man who adored her, but his brothers who respected and cared for her.

Her life, minus the life-threatening wounds and traumatic kidnapping, was what I wanted. That kind of dedication. That kind of love. I ignored the voice that told me I might not ever get it. The one that lectured me that my life choices, my place in the club, might rob me of that kind of respect. I pretended that voice didn't exist. Instead, I did what I always did, I had hope. Positivity that something great was around the corner.

And, at that moment in the middle of the night, when I was creeping out after falling asleep watching movies with Jagger—no funny business, much to my chagrin—I didn't expect to hit something that didn't mean happiness only heartbreak.

"Fuck a duck!" I yelled in fright as I half collided with a hard body while I was turning the corner to head out of the clubhouse.

I scuttled back about five feet when I realized who the hard body belonged to. Felt the heat of attraction that came with the contact.

Hansen and I stared at each other in the dim light, me trying to get my breathing under control.

We stayed like that for a moment, before I found my legs and a shaky smile. I walked my way toward him, trying to act like I hadn't almost climbed a wall to escape his heat. I had no choice, he was standing in front of the only exit. I'd only encountered him a couple of times since his harsh words, and I had vowed to put on a brave face and a smile next time I saw him.

"Where you going?" he barked.

He didn't seem to make any motion that he was going to move out of my way. I didn't want to get too close to him either. I felt like my body would betray just how much he affected me.

"Home," I whispered, on reflex.

His brows furrowed. "At fuckin' four in the morning?" he clipped.

"I wasn't planning on falling asleep, but Jagger insisted on watching a movie with subtitles, I need some magic and elves or interdimensional travel to keep me awake," I said slowly, trying to keep my tone light. "I've got projects I need to do. So I'm going home to brew a bucket of coffee and finish them," I continued, praying he'd let me past so I didn't have to struggle with his stare.

He didn't stop staring at me. I didn't miss the way his entire body hardened when I mentioned Jagger.

I loved this man. There wasn't anything for it. Ever since I first laid eyes on him, something in me stirred. It was him. The man for me. It wasn't just because he was hot. He was. His bald head showed off the fact he had a great shaped skull. A weird thing to notice, I know. It was smooth and accentuated his sharp bone structure and strong features. He wasn't hand-some. No, someone that masculine wasn't described as *hand-*

some. Something radiated off him that screamed *man.* Something in addition to his tall frame and hulking muscles. Something about the way he held himself and the way he walked. In the end, it was his eyes that trapped me. They were piercing blue, so piercing I felt them penetrate my soul. All I could ever think about was those hard, beautiful, eyes softening for me. For me and me only. That rigid form relaxing in my arms.

Only recently, with his painful dismissal, had I realized that would never happen.

"You're going home, in your neighborhood, at this fuckin' time?" he half growled, shaking me out of my fantasy.

"You know where I live?" I said by answer.

He was right. My neighborhood wasn't exactly Beverly Hills. Far from it. But, thanks to its less than stellar reputation, rent was cheap and I managed to get a decent sized house for less than a matchbox apartment in the 'better' part of town. I wasn't rolling in cash, but I wanted to make myself a home. Somewhere warm and welcoming. I'd grown up in an even rougher neighborhood and, in the two years I'd lived where I was, I'd been fine. That may have been because of my connection to the club. Even the stupidest criminals knew not to mess with the Sons of Templar. Even though I was only a club whore, I was their property, and no one damaged what belonged to the Sons unless they wanted their jaw wired shut.

I was surprised that Hansen knew where I lived. Even though I was secretly in love with him, he did not betray any interest in me or any of the girls. Well, until the kitchen episode.

"Fuckin' hell," he muttered, shaking his head.

My back reared up slightly. Maybe it was him treating me

like some kind of idiot for going home. I was a lot of things—I knew that—but an idiot was not one of them.

"I'm fine," I snapped. "I've rolled into my place hundreds of times, yet to be peppered with bullet holes or assaulted." My sarcasm and irritation shocked even me. I wasn't a grumpy person. Regardless of what shit was swirling in my life, I was happy. I didn't take shit from people, but I also didn't feed into shit. The girls around here said something nasty, I usually let it roll off my back. Life's too short to hold onto venom and let it settle. He seemed to bring it out in me.

Hansen's face turned to granite. "Do not..." he ground out, "...joke about shit like that." His voice was so full of ice I tried not to flinch.

"You gonna let me past?" I said finally, breaking our stare off.

He stepped forward, his hand going to gently touch my hair. I froze, barely being able to breathe at the gentle touch that contrasted the hard words he had uttered moments before.

"Your hair suits you," he murmured, staring at the spiky strands.

I didn't say anything, just in case I'd strayed into a parallel universe where the Hansen I knew was replaced with someone who actually liked me. Wanted me. I didn't want to upset the fragile balance.

The spell shattered when he sighed and stepped aside. I walked by him, trying not to inhale his musky scent, trying to ignore the tingles of having his body so close.

He surprised me by following me out to the parking lot, silently. I couldn't see him but I could feel him. I moved to face him when he mounted his bike, just as I made it to my car. Incidentally, it was parked right next to it.

"What are you doing?" I asked as he sat himself down.

He stared at me. "Making sure you get home all right," he replied tightly.

My eyes popped out. "You don't have to—"

"Get in the car, Mace," he interrupted.

"But seriously," I tried again.

"In the fuckin' car, babe," he ordered.

I stared at him for a moment. My eyes softened of their own accord. I let myself buy into the fantasy, just for a moment. The fantasy in which he cared for me, felt an iota of what I felt for him. That I was *his*, not just some club property that he was ensuring didn't get tainted. I let the warmness of that fantasy fill me up.

"Okay, honey," I said almost without realizing it. My tone had betrayed something, I knew because his framed jolted slightly and something moved in his features.

My face reddened and I quickly hopped in my car, not needing rejection or indifference to freeze the warmth in my belly.

The headlights followed me all the way home. And then, when I got out of my shitty Corolla and walked into my reasonably nice house in my shitty neighborhood, he sat on his bike and I didn't hear him leave until I was safely inside.

I tried to hold onto the warmth, but it seemed to ride away with him.

THREE

"What have you done to your hair? You look like a lesbian."
My grandmother's body may have been succumbing to old age,
but her mouth would be sharp as ever until the day she died.

I sighed and let the comment roll over me. I liked my pixie
cut. My hairdresser had cut my chocolate hair into the spiky
'do a couple of weeks ago. I'd been dubious at first, but it suited
my small face, made my brown eyes seem bigger and it didn't
need any fuss in the morning, a total plus.

"How are you liking this new place?" I asked, ignoring her.
It was the best policy.

She screwed up her perfectly made up face. Despite being
in a shoebox room, she'd placed a mirror on each wall and put a
vanity cabinet in the room, complete with her brush and
makeup set. You almost had to walk sideways to get in, and we
were squished sitting on the bed. She didn't seem to mind, so I
didn't comment.

"They're imbeciles, every one of them," she declared
loudly, despite the open door.

I sighed. *Here we go.*

"Why I had to be shoved in this tiny place full of drooling morons, I have no clue. Don't you care about your grandmother at all?" she shot at me, venom in her tone.

I did. For some insane reason. The woman who'd raised me with insults and bitterness still somehow held a place in my heart.

"You know I care, Grandma, this place is much better than what you could've had, we're lucky your insurance got you this," I repeated like I did every time I was here.

She narrowed her eyes. "I don't need to be here. You just shoved me away so you can have your loose lifestyle and hang out with drug dealers and miscreants. How I raised such a brazen hussy is beyond me."

Half an hour. I'd had half an hour without her bringing up what a disappointment I was. *A record.*

I did my best for the rest of the visit to grit my teeth and smile through the barbs. I'd done it for eighteen years, I could do it for fifteen more minutes.

I sucked in a huge breath of air once I got outside.

"Freedom!" I declared, holding my arms out dramatically.

I heard a chuckle from beside me and I moved my head to the source.

An attractive man wearing a dress shirt, unbuttoned at the collar and casual slacks was smiling at me. His hair was cut and styled within an inch of its life, and his face was classically handsome and clean shaven. His smile was warm and reached his eyes.

"It's a bit like that in there, isn't it?" He nodded his head at the double doors of the assisted living facility. "Sucks all the happiness out of you as soon as you walk through those doors."

"Yeah, it's not somewhere I'll ever be spending my twilight years, that's for sure. I'd rather something more comfortable, like a POW camp," I replied, shivering at the thought.

"Grandparents?" he guessed, moving closer.

"Grandmother... spawn of Satan... she answers to either one," I told him seriously.

He chuckled again, it was throaty and easy. *Genuine.*

"Seems that this place has the ability to turn people into that," he said with a twinkle in his eye.

I shook my head. "Oh no, she'd embraced the dark side long before that," I told him. "I think she made a deal with the Dark Prince in the womb," I continued.

He grinned at me. "I'd make a deal with the devil to make sure I never end up somewhere like that," he said lightly.

I nodded. "I feel you, dude. I'd rather wax my legs with duct tape for the rest of my life than entertain the possibly of living in a place cloaked in death."

He chuckled, *again*, to my shock. I didn't expect such a straight-laced looking guy to be entertained by my word vomit.

"I'm Robert, by the way," he introduced himself, stepping closer.

I smiled at him. Mostly because I wasn't getting a creepy vibe, and I doubted he was about to assault or kidnap me outside an old folks' home. That and his eyes seemed sad. He needed someone to smile at him

"Macy," I said. "Though they refer to me in the *House of Death* as the World's Biggest Disappointment," I joked.

"I think I'll stick with Macy. Want to grab a drink? Shake off the feeling of death?" he suggested lightly.

Wow. He was not only entertained, but asking me out— outside a nursing home, no less. Somehow he pulled it off.

I looked at him. The promise of easy conversation and maybe even something more was implied. Thanks to the fact he was easy on the eyes and actually had a sense of humor, despite the straight-laced appearance. Maybe we'd hit it off? Go on more dates. Have decidedly polite sex where he'd make sure I was satisfied. He'd take me out of my shitty neighborhood, my nicely decorated but shabby house, to a McMansion in the suburbs. Have two point five kids and a dog. A nice life for some. Not for me.

Maybe all of that wouldn't come from one simple date? Maybe I'd like him? But I was sure he wouldn't like me, not after he found out who I really was.

I smiled at him. "Sorry, I'm kind of spoken for," I said. I was, in a sense. Just by an entire motorcycle club who considered me *club property* and all treated me as such, albeit with respect. Not something this guy would exactly understand.

His face fell slightly but still kept his easy smile. "That ever changes, or you just need some company after an ordeal in there... I'm here every Saturday. Same time," he told me kindly.

I smiled. "I'll keep that in mind."

Walking to my car I tried to shake off Grandma's insults, attempting to entertain the idea of one day saying yes to a man who lived on the right side of the law, who held the promise of something normal. I couldn't picture it.

ARIANNE: *Come to The Rock now, bitch. Drinks on me.*

. . .

ARIANNE WASN'T a full-time club girl, just hung around when she felt like it. She didn't belong to any of the guys and was happy with that arrangement. She went through some shit as a kid, shit that made her run as fast as her platforms would take her from any form of commitment. That's why being a casual club girl appealed to her. We'd known each other since we were strippers at the same bar together and just clicked. We've been basically inseparable ever since. If I wasn't at the club, or working, I was with her.

I looked down at my attire—white cut-offs, a white lace cami and a black and white floaty kimono over the top. My slouchy black ankle boots had a high heel, I'd picked them up at a vintage shop and they were my favorite pair. I never dressed down when I was visiting my grandmother, it was a silent form of rebellion. She had informed me I looked like a streetwalker today. Streetwalker chic was perfect for The Rock. It was what most people would call rough, on the outskirts of town and there was an unspoken rule that it was the Son's bar. People from town came every now and then, mostly those who wanted in with the club, or girls wanting to take a walk on the wild side. That was fine. Most got scared away, but some stayed. But no other club was welcome, apart from those that got an invitation. Or those who wanted to start a war.

I PULLED up to the bar beside the bikes I recognized, and breathed a sigh of relief when I walked through the door.

"Macey Moo!" was shouted across the bar .

Arianne bounded over to me, two shots in her hands. She

gave me one. "Knew you'd need about five of these after an hour with Satan's Mistress," she said knowingly.

I clinked my glass to hers and downed the bitter liquid welcoming the burn.

She knew me too well.

We linked arms and made it over to a table that was crowded with a few men from the club. I got a chorus of male hellos and some chin lifts. Scarlett gave me a look and I rolled my eyes and blew her a kiss. Despite herself, she smiled slightly. She wasn't a complete bitch, I knew that fact. Life hadn't exactly been easy on any of the women who found themselves connected to the club. Scarlett was no exception. She was beautiful, her blonde hair tumbled down her back, her full curves were in all the right places. And were currently on display in a leather miniskirt and white tee that barely brushed the top of her ribcage. All that, plus her makeup was there to make sure you didn't miss her, but also to hide something else. It was her eyes, though, they betrayed the demons of her past. Demons I knew haunted her, but to which she wouldn't admit. She liked people to think she was hard and nothing bothered her. Only someone who was trying to do the same would notice.

The men seemed keyed up, so they drank more than usual. I thought it might have been because of the drama of the past few days. Amy and the Cali boys had left yesterday, things seemed wired around the club. I didn't mind they had decided to turn to alcohol to treat whatever had them so tightly wound. Arianne was right. I needed alcohol to wash off the bitterness that came with my visit to my grandmother.

"Get me a beer, Macy," Hammer barked at me after I had downed a couple more shots.

I stood, not giving him any shit like I might have the others. That was because Hammer was one of the few in the MC that treated me like I *was* a second-class citizen because I had a vagina. He was cold, and I never really liked him. But, he was a Son and therefore, part of the family. So I complied, walking to the bar.

I nodded to the bartender, who knew who I was and what I wanted. He gave me a chin lift from the other end where he was serving a customer. I leaned against the bar to wait, and that was when everything seemed to turn quiet. Quiet, with these guys, usually meant bad. I'd been with the club long enough to know that. This quiet was because of the three men who had walked into the bar, standing not too far away from me. I didn't recognize them, but their shaved heads and a disgusting tattoo publicized the fact they were hateful supremacists communicated they were not in the right place. *At all.*

Hammer and Levi pushed out of their seats along with Gary, the Prospect, yet to earn his road name.

"Think you've taken a wrong turn on the way to Nazi-town, fucker," Hammer spat, hatefully.

One of the men, with a tattoo marring half his face, scowled at Hammer. Then his eyes moved to Gary. Gary was a new Prospect but well liked, despite the constant hazing he endured. Gary was handsome, in a way that made me think he could have been a male model, in case *outlaw* didn't work out for him. Gary was also African American.

The bigot's face turned into a sneer and he spat at his feet. That gesture, and just being who they were, was enough provocation for Gary to push his fist into the tattooed face. Of course, then everyone got involved in a tangle of arms and punches.

I wasn't the hugest fan of violence, but being connected to the club, I'd seen my fair share. I'm pretty sure the Sons probably had a special account to pay for the repairs which would be needed after this brawl, evidenced by the fact Hammer slammed someone into a table. I did have some kind of satisfaction watching those animals get pummeled.

My eyes flicked from the growing brawl to the door, even amongst the chaos, I could feel him. *Hansen.* His blank eyes flipped over the fight with disinterest, then they found mine. They did what they always did, froze me in place. This time, though, they widened in something akin to concern. His frame moved slightly and he yelled something I couldn't hear over the music and carnage.

Then, a hard body slammed into me, sending me flying. I wasn't curvy or tall like the other girls. I didn't just wear heels to complete my outfits, it was also to give me the illusion of height. That's why the force of such a large and hard body slamming into mine sent me hurtling into a table, which overturned and pain exploded in my head as it hit the dirty floor. I vaguely worried about the fate of my white outfit before I drifted off.

"YOU GUYS FUCKIN' think to consider your goddamn surroundings when throwing a punch?" an angry voice yelled.

My head throbbed so I didn't try to move too much at this point, nor open my eyes.

"She's fuckin' tiny, bro. How the fuck were we meant to

even realize she was there?" a voice argued, sounding slightly apologetic.

"Bitch should've gotten out of the way," another, non-apologetic voice added.

Arms around me tightened, and even with my eyes closed and my mind rather foggy, I could feel the air turn electric.

"You better back the fuck off and shut that mouth, Hammer," a beautiful voice, laden with fury said.

I fluttered my eyes and saw I was up in the air, and a familiar stubbled jaw was tight with what I recognized as anger. Then, it moved and eyes settled in on me. Eyes that immediately softened.

I lost my breath.

"Babe." he murmured. "You okay?"

I rubbed my head slightly and flinched at the pain. "Yeah, think so, despite having said goodbye to some brain cells." I looked around to see a huddle of hard but concerned faces. Well, apart from Hammer, who was scowling. "Why do you boys punch each other when this is what it feels like? Stupid if you ask me," I muttered, and there were a few chuckles.

"She's fine. She can still use that smart mouth, means no lasting brain damage," Levi joked.

Hansen, interestingly, didn't find anything funny. He stepped forward and the men seemed to disperse, Levi giving Hansen a knowing grin. Jagger gave me a long look before he turned back to the table. The skinheads were nowhere to be found.

"You can put me down now," I told him, confused as to why we were heading toward the exit. I also didn't actually want him to put me down, *like ever*, but I knew it was necessary. I didn't want to get used to his arms around me. False hope and all that.

Hansen ignored me, continuing toward the door.

"Seriously, a beer and a subsequent shot will fix me right up," I lied, ignoring the pain.

Hansen glanced down at me. "Jesus," he shook his head. "Even a blow to the head can't shake the nut outta you." His face hardened. "You're not staying here, and you sure as shit aren't having anymore to drink."

His boots crunched on the gravel as he directed us toward a bike. *His bike.*

He gently, more gently than I ever thought possible, set me on my feet.

I swayed slightly and his large hands spanned my waist to settle me.

He frowned down at me for a moment.

"You drive here?" he asked after a second.

I blinked away the stars in front of my vision. "Yeah...my purse," I said slowly, realizing it was most likely still slung over the back of a chair in the bar.

Hansen proved me wrong on that score, dangling it from his hand.

"You carried my purse?" I said in wonder. "The big, bad, macho biker carried my fringed and decidedly fabulous bag while carrying me?" I clarified. "Wow," I said when his face stayed blank. "I'm surprised that it didn't like... burst into flames on account of it not being able to be held by such a testosterone-infused creature."

Hansen looked at me a moment and smiled slightly. "Fuckin' hell," he muttered to himself. "Keys, get them," he continued, thrusting the bag at me.

I took it and got my keys, out of reflex. That was because Hansen's face had an easy, almost amused look painted on it. His eyes were warm and concern danced underneath it. It was all for *me*.

I didn't care if a head injury was responsible for these hallucinations, I was rolling with it.

He took them and directed me by the waist to my car. I looked longingly over my shoulder at his sleek Harley. My desire to ride pressed up against him almost trumped my thumping headache. *Almost*.

He unlocked the car and gently pushed me into the passenger seat. Still dumbstruck by his demeanor, I did this silently. He got into my car and I restrained a snort at how weird the big biker looked in my shitty car. *How out of place*.

"What are you doing?" I asked, finally finding my voice.

He looked over at me. "Seatbelt," he commanded.

I ignored him. "Seriously, I'm feeling much better now. I can drive myself home, and you don't have to subject yourself to the horror of driving something that isn't your beautiful Harley."

Crap. Did I just say beautiful Harley? I was a dork.

Hansen raised an eyebrow, and his eyes danced slightly. "Seatbelt," he repeated, this time, his voice was lighter.

I complied, more out of embarrassment from my stupid mouth than anything else. Once I had done so, we reversed out of the lot.

"Macy," he murmured, finally gaining my attention from the window. I'd really wanted to imprint every inch of him driving my car on my memory, but I refrained. It would only serve as torture when he went back to indifference.

"Next time I'm on my bike, only thing that'll be making it

beautiful, is the fact you're on the back of it," he informed me, his voice rough.

I succeeded in keeping my mouth shut at his words, but I didn't succeed in masking my expression. Did that mean what I thought it meant? *'Back of my bike'* was kind of a declaration in this world. One that I had dreamed of Hansen coming out with. Maybe a head injury made me imagine things. He couldn't seriously be saying this. Not after the actions that had bruised my soul. The ones that had communicated he wanted me as far away from the back of his bike as possible. Those words contradicted all of that and made my stomach jump.

He didn't seem to require my answer because his attention went back to the road. We were silent for a while. Me, because I was trying to control my emotions and not let that feeling of warmth spread at that simple sentence. Too good to be true meant it probably was. I was an optimist but also a realist.

I finally noted our surroundings. Instead of taking the turn back into town, Hansen had followed the road that led out into the desert where houses were randomly dotted amongst the dry landscape.

"Um, this isn't the way to my house," I muttered.

Hansen's eyes stayed on the road. "I know. We're going to my place," he declared.

I stared at his jaw. "Your place?" I almost squeaked.

He nodded.

Holy shit.

I FOUGHT the heaviness that seemed to be dragging down my eyelids. It hadn't been long since Hansen had declared our destination, only about fifteen minutes, but the journey of the car and the desolate landscape seemed to serve as a sort of lullaby.

"Macy," Hansen's voice cut through the silence.

I jolted upright, my eyes blinking away the fuzziness.

His hand went to my jaw and turned it to face him. "Don't fall asleep," he commanded with concern.

I stared at him. "How much longer to your place?" I finally asked, when his hand dropped from my jaw and the moment was lost.

He nodded to a dirt road to our left and the car slowed down. "'Bout a minute."

We traveled down the road, and a small but well-kept house was illuminated by his headlights, the sun just starting to disappear. It had a flat roof and was light brown, the clay-like outside similar to many houses around here. It surprised me.

"This is your place?" I asked as we parked in front of a garage.

"Yep," he replied.

"Doesn't your bike get dirty, traveling down that road?" I nodded my head in the direction we had just come.

He looked at me a moment, a strange expression on his face. Then he shook his head and got out of the car. I took that as my cue to follow suit. Being vertical so abruptly made the ground seem to sway, so I steadied myself on the car. Before I knew it, Hansen's hands were around me, lifting me into his arms.

"You don't need to carry me bodily, I was just catching my bearings," I protested weakly, my head throbbing.

Hansen ignored me and walked us into his house. The

cool, fresh air assaulted me as soon as we walked in, it was a welcoming chill from the hot sticky climate.

I didn't get to inspect much as Hansen quickly walked us through his open plan living room and into a hallway. I spotted a leather sofa and armchair, and a huge television, not much else. His hallway was devoid of pictures—devoid of any personality. The same could be said about his room. He walked us in, a nearly made bed displaying a gray bedspread and dark wooden headboard—it was meticulously tidy. He deposited me gently on his soft bed, his hand tenderly brushing my forehead.

"Stay there," he commanded softly.

I couldn't do anything but nod and he disappeared. I looked around his bedroom, other than the huge bed, there was a set of drawers, a door leading to what I guessed was a bathroom and smaller double doors of a closet. The items on his dresser were lined up tidily, and there was only a framed picture of the Sons emblem on the wall. I knew he was in the military, which was probably why this place was so gosh darned tidy, but that didn't explain why it didn't have anything other than the bare necessities.

He would have hated my room. I was far from tidy. My bed was more often than not unmade, my walls were covered with pictures, places I wanted to go, snaps of Arianne and me, and a couple of me and the boys from the club. It was full of knick-knacks, shit that didn't serve a purpose but looked cute. I wanted my personality to bleed into my home, wanted it to reflect me. Hansen obviously didn't agree with that decorating idea.

What felt like seconds later, he appeared with a little torch and one of his hands rested gentled at the side of my head.

"Gonna shine this in your eyes, babe," he told me in a brisk tone.

I squinted slightly at the light. Then I did as he instructed, looking various ways.

He clicked it off, seeming satisfied. His eyes still held a note of concern.

"You feeling sick? Any numbness?" he asked, his voice brisk.

I shook my head, remembering Hansen's history as a medic in the military.

"Okay, good. You tell me if you start feeling either of those things," he said firmly.

I nodded again.

"You tired?" he asked.

I took stock of myself, then glanced at the clock beside the bed. It was just after ten. I was a night owl, so this was seriously early for me, but the knock on the head had me quite drowsy.

"Not really," I lied, not wanting to waste my time in what I deduced was Hansen's bed unconscious.

He gave me a look that said he didn't believe me but didn't say anything. He moved to grab a remote then turned on the flat screen across the room. It was big, like the one in his living room.

"Got movies and shit on here," he told me gruffly.

Then, because it seemed like his goal of the night was to shake an already shaken brain, he lifted me and moved me slightly so he could lie on the bed and tuck me into his shoulder.

I stared at the cords of his neck in amazement.

I was snuggling... with Hansen... on his bed... watching

movies! Granted I was suffering from a head injury, but that didn't matter hugely at that moment.

"Babe..." he muttered, flicking through the channels, "... eyes required to be on the screen to pick a movie."

I kept staring, imprinting this moment into my memory. "I think I'm happy with where my eyes are right now," I whispered, deciding a head injury took away what little filter I had. And any sense of self-preservation.

His body tightened. His eyes didn't move from the screen. "Macy. You're hurt. Which means, as much as I would like to do otherwise, only thing we can do right now is watch a movie. So pick a fuckin' movie," he said tightly.

His voice was harsh but the meaning behind it wasn't. My stomach jumped and with effort, I tore my gaze away from his handsome face and proceeded to pick a movie. One that Hansen groaned and teased me about, but watched nonetheless. I wouldn't know how much he actually watched, considering I passed out in the first fifteen minutes, despite my efforts to suck as much time out of this moment as I could.

FOUR

I woke up feeling warm. Really warm. That was because I was quite literally tangled up with Hansen. I blinked a couple of times, just to make sure I wasn't in some super realistic, superbly amazing, yet PG fantasy. *Nope.* This was real. I was actually half lying on his chest, my leg draped over his thighs. His corded arms were tightly coiled around my shoulder and waist. He did literally smell like a delicious mix of sexy and masculine.

My shoes and kimono had been taken off at some point during the night and I was only in my shorts and cami.

I ignored the pounding in my skull. I'd take twelve rounds with Tyson if this was what I got in return. My eyes trailed across his chest, which was bare.

I repeat—bare.

His pecs were defined like they'd been sculpted out of clay and his chest was positively the best I'd ever laid eyes on. It was also devoid of tattoos, apart from one over the top of his heart, the words '*Semper Fidelis*' scrawled over the top of a cross and dagger. I frowned at a scar on his chest, then moved my gaze. His shoulders were naked of ink also, which I was glad of. Who needed to ink over muscled perfection?

I moved up slightly so I could look over his sleeping face. With the relaxation of slumber, his normally tight face was soft and blank. I lifted up, unable to help myself, touching my lips to his softly. Even if this was the only moment I got, I was going to make sure I made the most of it. My movement caused his body to tighten and his arms moved so I was positioned entirely on top of him, his hard-on pressing into me. Desire pooled in my stomach. My lips, which were positioned close-mouthed on his, were suddenly set on fire. His mouth moved with mine, moving past the tender peck I'd intended, to a full on kiss. It was a kiss that I'd been imagining, dreaming of, ever since he'd given me a taste a week ago. One that seemed to surpass every one of my expectations and go right up there with Leo and Kate as one of the best kisses in history.

He abruptly disengaged, and his face turned tight. His eyes were flaming with desire, but his jaw hardened and his neck pulsed with restraint.

"You're hurt," he clipped, his voice rough.

"I'm fine," I protested, leaning forward. I'd have to be bleeding from a stab wound to not capitalize on the fact he had seemed to forget about the fact he wasn't interested in me. I would regret it later when he finally dropped me, but I was all about instant gratification.

He held my head gently, but putting enough pressure so my lips couldn't meet his.

"You're testing every inch of my restraint right now, Mace. And I'll tell you, it's almost in fuckin' tatters after only tasting that mouth once in the year I've been dreaming about it," he growled. "And it tastes a fuck of a lot sweeter than I remember." His eyes darkened. "I remember honey, baby."

Every part of my body seemed to turn to jelly at his words, and my panties dampened at the sex in his tone and in his eyes. I didn't even register the allusion to the fact he'd been holding himself back for a year, I just attacked.

This time his gentle hold wasn't enough to stop my mouth from hitting his, and he seemed to pause for a split second before returning my furious kiss with an intensity that rivaled the one moments before.

He flipped me on my back, his hard body pressing into mine, almost drowning me in muscle. My legs went around his waist, needing friction, needing his body as close as humanly possible.

He yanked back from my mouth, his eyes clouded over. "You need to tell me right fuckin' now if we gotta stop, babe. 'Cause after this moment, I ain't gonna be able to," he informed me tightly.

"Only thing I want you to stop doing is talking," I ordered huskily, needing him inside me, like yesterday. Or more accurately a year ago.

He searched my face for a split second then his mouth went back for another brutal, beautiful assault. His hands running up and down my sides, moving to cup my breasts. I made a little sound in his mouth at the contact.

His body was gone from mine, I was about to protest when his hands went to my cami.

"Arms up," he ordered.

I complied, watching him through my lashes. He let out a hiss when I unclasped my lacy bra once he'd thrown my cami aside. His reaction to my bare breasts made my already damp panties drenched with need. He pushed me back on the bed and his mouth fastened on my nipple.

I gasped at the feeling, running my hands over his smooth head. His hands moved to my shorts, undoing them quickly, and yanking them off my body, my panties going with them. His attention moved to my clit, I gasped, almost climaxing from the contact of his callused fingers.

"Fuckin' drenched," he bit out, eyes never leaving mine.

Hansen stood, and I watched as he divested himself of his jeans, revealing him in all of his magnificent glory. He reached to his bedside table, grabbing a condom and quickly sheathing himself.

The act of him doing that—of watching him while keeping his eyes firmly on me was hands down the most erotic thing I'd ever witnessed.

Then he was on top of me, everything seemed to fall away, apart from his body on mine. His eyes keeping me captive. He gently ran his hand over the top of my forehead. "You good baby?" he asked in a tone that juxtaposed the furious need blazing in his eyes.

That moment was one that required brutal honesty. "I'm the best I've ever been in my entire life," I whispered.

His body jolted slightly, his eyes flaring. Then, he was inside me. Filling me. Consuming me. Every stroke that built me up was also a stroke I treasured. The feeling of him inside me, his body pressing into mine. The fact that his eyes stared into me, with that tenderness I yearned for from the moment I laid eyes on him. If this were all we'd ever have, I'd cradle that memory until the end of my days. This wasn't fucking like it was with anyone in the club, this was something else. Something deeper.

He flipped us, so I was on top, straddling him. His hands went to my hips.

"Want to watch you ride me, baby," he growled. His hand moved to cup my breast.

So I did. I rode him, not slow and gentle like it had been before. Fast and furious and chasing the climax I knew would shatter my world. The whole time, my eyes didn't leave the face of the man I'd been in love with for a year.

It hit me. Like a ton of bricks, an explosion of fireworks. My entire body shuddered on top of him as I rode the waves of desire. I vaguely registered Hansen flipping us back over while I clutched onto his back, scratching his skin as he prolonged my ecstasy by slamming into me hard and brutal.

He made a sound signifying his own release, his mouth inches from mine.

We stayed frozen, breathing heavily. I searched his face, letting the beauty of the moment sink into my soul. His hand traced my lips lightly.

"That..." he began roughly, "...was the beginning of me being the only man to possess that sweet pussy. The only man who sinks into that tight velvet," he declared firmly. "That..." he continued, "...was me finally claiming what's mine."

I blinked at his words, my heart soaring, but being unable to fathom it. "It's always been yours," I whispered, sounding like a lovestruck idiot, but not giving a shit.

He blinked, then moved to claim my mouth.

We didn't speak for a long while after that.

"TAKE THESE," Hansen commanded, dropping two pills into my hands.

We were standing in his small, but impressive kitchen. Me with wet hair, both sipping coffee. I was wearing one of his tees, which reached almost my knees. He was wearing jeans, the top two buttons undone.

I struggled to move my eyes away from his defined 'v' and dark hair peeking out from below.

"Usually, I only take E at raves and dubstep concerts, but okay dude," I told him seriously, shrugging my shoulders.

He smirked in response.

I took the pills, washing them down with my coffee.

His hands stroked my spiky hair gently. "You in much pain, baby?"

I still wasn't used to his gentle words and the fact he was touching me with such tenderness, so it took me a moment to register his question. "Nah, nothing I can't handle," I replied honestly.

He gave me a look, then jerked his head to the breakfast bar. "Sit, I'll make you breakfast." He kissed me firmly before patting my ass and turning to his fridge.

I padded wordlessly around the kitchen island and moved to perch on one of his stools. I swiveled to admire the view his sliding doors had of the dry and rolling landscape. Not another house was in sight and it seemed like we were in the middle of nowhere, the only two people left on the planet. I swiveled the chair back to an arguably better view. Hansen's back, which was not only corded and muscly, but covered in the club's insignia. I struggled not to drool into my coffee.

We didn't speak for a few minutes, the sizzling of the pan and clanging of pots and bowls serving as the only noise. It wasn't an uncomfortable silence, but I wasn't one to do well with not speaking for long periods of time. I also, it seemed, wasn't one to revel in a moment I had been dreaming of for a year.

"What gives?" I asked suddenly.

Hansen turned his head around, raising his brow in silent question.

"Well..." I continued, "...you don't seem to show any interest in anyone. Then you corner me in the kitchen last week and kiss the shit out of me. *Then* inform me you don't want me. Then this..." I waved my hands between us. After my mind caught up with my mouth, I mentally chastised myself. Could I not just revel in the moment of relative domestic bliss with the man I'd been pining over? No. Me and my stupid mouth had to question the why of it, potentially setting flames to it all.

Hansen's face hardened and he turned his attention back to the stove, moving the pans from the heat. Then he rounded the counter and moved my stool so he was standing in front of me. His hands framed my face.

"Just 'cause I didn't show any interest in you doesn't mean I wasn't interested, Macy," he said softly. "I was. Fascinated in fact, by this girl who seemed to radiate happiness and goodness. This girl didn't belong in the life she'd chosen, she deserved something more, something better." He searched my face. "So I waited for her to realize that. For her to see her kind heart and gentle soul would get trampled if she stayed. But I lost my restraint, my willpower, that night I saw you dancing like you didn't have a care in the world, like your life was sunshine and rainbows."

He played with my hair. "Been punishing myself for doing

that, babe. For getting a taste of something, I shouldn't have let myself have. Last night, watching you get thrown across the room like a fuckin' rag doll," his jaw hardened, "I decided I wasn't waiting anymore. You gonna stick with this life, you're going to do it belonging to me. I'll make sure nothing tramples over you, ruins the goodness that's endured."

I blinked at him. This was all moving at the speed of light. I felt like I'd just won the emotional lottery. How could getting knocked out at a biker bar equate to getting everything you'd always wanted?

I swallowed. "It doesn't bother you..." I started carefully, "...that I've been with..." I started to voice my hidden fear, needing to know now if the position I'd chosen in the club was going to make him think of me in that way forever.

He silenced me by pressing his hand to my lips, his eyes hardening. "Yeah, it bothers me," he clipped tightly.

My heart fell.

"That I was pursuing some fucked up reasoning, and by doing that, all my brothers in the club got a taste of what I've always considered mine," he continued. "Lost sleep over that fuckin' shit. Almost lost my mind..." He paused, his hand moving from my lip to my jaw. "Do I think of you any differently? No babe. That shit was on me. You'll always be the girl that radiates happiness and goodness, the one with no fuckin' filter, and a brain that comes out with craziest of shit." The hands at my jaw tightened. "My girl," he finished.

Yep. Emotional lottery. In the billions.

"You told them that?" I deduced. "That's why no one has so much as checked out my ass in the past week and a half?"

Hansen's gaze turned blank. "Trust me, babe, even when I threaten them with death and dismemberment, they ain't gonna stop checkin' out that perky ass," he stated flatly. His hand moved to trace my lip. "Moment I tasted the sweetness, realized it was better than I ever could have imagined, was the moment I knew no one else was tasting that shit again."

I jolted. "So you scared them all off, even though you decided to push me away?" I said sharply. Even though his words were sweet, I couldn't help but be irritated. He may have been trying to protect me from his big, bad, biker world, but that wasn't his decision to make. I chose to be in this world. I wanted it. I was getting mighty sick of people deciding the only place I felt I belonged wasn't right for me.

Hansen sighed. "I was trying to make sure I didn't commit murder," he stated. "'Cause that's what I would've done, had someone touched what I had finally tasted after a year, brother or not."

I sucked in a breath. "If you felt this way, why in the heck did you push me away, you big idiot?" I asked, smacking his shoulder. "You had to have known I'd be yours, the moment your mouth touched mine," I said quieter, losing my bravado.

He did that thing, that thing where his eyes swam the depths of my soul. "Yeah babe, I knew. Which was why I pushed you away. If I didn't claim you like I have now, I knew I'd never let you go, let you have the chance of a better life."

My heart pounded in my chest. "And now?" I breathed.

"And now, I'm the one that's going to give it to you," he declared. "That answer your question?"

"I think that answers that question and any question I could have about anything anywhere in the universe... ever," I said stupidly.

Hansen grinned. He kissed my head gently and went back to the grill.

My fantasy turned reality stayed firmly in place as he cooked us a delicious breakfast, which we ate on his patio. It then continued after we finished said breakfast and had sex on his breakfast bar. And sofa.

The whole day was spent discovering each other's bodies, whispering stupid jokes—me, and laughing at stupid jokes—Hansen. Despite a nagging headache, which Hansen was very vigilant about, it was almost the best day in my life to date. Actually, it was the best day of my life to date. Period.

LATE ON SUNDAY AFTERNOON, I was loath to break the spell that had tangled itself around us. I really didn't want to go back to my chicly decorated but shabby house and sit in front of a computer screen for the next four hours. I wanted to cuddle up to a warm yet firm body and continue to spend time in Hansen's sparsely decorated but decidedly not shabby house. I also didn't want to leave this house. I was terrified of doing so, I'd break whatever spell we were under and reality would come hurtling back in, or maybe Ashton Kutcher would come running in with a camera crew declaring this whole wonderful day an elaborate trick.

I reasoned my emotional trauma would make for great television. As would Hansen's abs.

I trailed his pec, touching the light puckered scar marring an otherwise smooth and perfect torso. "What's this from?" I asked quietly, giving myself five more minutes until I let reality back in.

"Bullet wound," he said in a distracted voice, his hands drawing light designs on my back.

I lifted my head to rest my chin on his chest, horrified. "Bullet wound?" I repeated.

He nodded nonchalantly like a bullet wound was something akin to a paper cut.

"You're telling me that this..." I touched the scar lightly, "... is evidence of a bullet tearing through your chest?" I asked, slightly hysterical.

"Missed anything major, babe. No biggy," he replied, eyes on me.

"No biggy?" I repeated. "The man classifies a gunshot wound as *'no biggy'* and he thinks I'm crazy," I addressed the empty room.

Hansen's chest vibrated as he chuckled. He lifted me so my body was fully on top of his and my face was almost touching his.

"Long time ago, Mace. Another life," he said, more seriously. "One that made me who I am. One that taught me a lot of shit. And one that I'm glad to be out of, on account of the high probably of getting shot."

I chewed all of this over. I imagined Hansen, big, strong, unflappable Hansen getting plowed down by a bullet. My stomach clenched tightly at the thought. I couldn't imagine him in a hospital bed.

"Please tell me you didn't dig the bullet out yourself, *rub some dirt on it* and run that beautiful butt right back into whatever situation got you shot in the first place?" I said with a hint of seriousness, but mostly joking.

Hansen smiled again. "No. I let someone who wasn't bleeding from the chest take the bullet out, and it took me a few weeks to get back on my feet."

"A few weeks? Geez okay, *Clark Kent.* I'm pretty sure it

would take *months* to get back on those glorious legs if you were anything less than superhuman," I teased.

"Glorious legs?" he repeated with a full grin.

I shrugged my shoulders. "You obviously don't skip leg day."

Hansen's face turned serious and he shook his head. "Christ, I'm a stupid fuck," he said. "Missing out on a woman who can make me laugh about a fuckin' gunshot wound and make me hard as stone at the same time," he muttered to himself. His hand trailed my collarbone. "Been missin' out, Mace, which means I've gotta lot of time to make up for."

I blinked away the slight prickling in my eyes at that statement and let myself wonder how such a switch had been flicked in the last twenty-four hours to turn Hansen into this. Soft eyes, smiles, heartfelt declarations littered with profanities.

I decided not to question it. When you looked too closely at things, you usually found out shit that you didn't want to know.

"Can you make up for it after you drop me home and let me chain myself to my computer?" I asked lightly, hating that his jaw turned hard at my request. "I'm on deadline for a couple of projects that need to be done by tomorrow," I told him apologetically. As much as I wanted to stay, I also had to eat. And buy shoes.

"Fuck," he muttered under his breath. "Don't like you in that neighborhood, babe," he said, repeating his sentiments of the other night.

As much as I liked his concern, I also felt slightly miffed at the unspoken fact that I, as a woman, couldn't take care of herself because suddenly I was attached to a macho biker.

I reared back slightly, Hansen's hands made it impossible to completely move off him.

"I feel like we had this conversation the other night. The neighborhood may not be winning any awards for the friendliest street in New Mexico, but no pipe bombs have been detonated there lately either," I retorted with sharp sarcasm.

"We had that particular conversation when you weren't mine. You are now," Hansen replied with a frown.

I narrowed my eyes. "Me becoming *yours* does not automatically transform me into a helpless damsel unable to function in the real world without an alpha biker at her back," I told him. "I've navigated the real world pretty darn well for twenty-four years. I'm tougher than I look," I finished. I wasn't too hot on telling him all the grim details of my bleak experience of the horrors of the real world, so I left it at that.

Hansen's face hardened. "Yeah babe, I don't doubt it. Being mine doesn't mean you can't handle the real world, just means now I can try my fuckin' best to protect you from it," he told me with determination.

I softened slightly. I couldn't help it. "How about you try and protect me from it, and also get right with the fact that doesn't include lecturing me about my zip code," I said gently, but firmly.

Hansen stared at me a moment. "You got beer at your place?" he asked weirdly.

I nodded.

"Cable?" he continued.

I nodded again.

"Right," he said, knifing up, and taking me with him.

He set us both on our feet and turned to his dresser.

I watched his back, confused. Then I got distracted at the

fluidity of the movement of his defined muscles, making the rider on his tattoo look like he was alive.

He turned after he had yanked on some faded jeans. Commando.

I licked my lips.

He stepped forward, grabbing my hips tightly. "You can't do that shit, Mace," he murmured.

I looked up at him. "What shit?"

"Kind of shit that makes me want to throw you back on that bed and bury myself in your pussy," he replied in a gravelly voice.

I swallowed. I so wanted him to do that. I struggled to remember why he couldn't.

"You got deadlines, remember?" he reminded me. "Now, I don't give a fuck about deadlines..." he continued, pulling my body flush to his, "...but you seemed mighty concerned about them before."

"Yes," I said shakily. "They're important." I was talking to myself more than him.

"Get dressed then," he ordered softly, turning back around.

"You don't need to get dressed," I pointed out, moving to locate my clothes. "I'm quite capable of driving myself."

Someone had dropped off his bike earlier today, I wasn't sure who, since Hansen had met them outside and I'd stayed in bed under his orders. Not that I could have moved at that moment, my body had been turned to jelly after too many orgasms.

"Don't want you driving babe, not after last night. Reaction times are delayed after any blow to the head," he told my back. "I'm drivin' you."

He was the medic, I guessed. "How will you get home?" I argued, yanking my cami over my head.

"Not planning on going home," he told me, slipping on his boots.

"You're not?" I repeated.

He shook his head. "Haven't got my fill of you yet, baby, not for today at least. So I'll drink some beers, watch the game, you do what you need to do. After that, I'll fuck you, then we'll go to sleep," he told me.

I stared at him, hoping he couldn't see my belly doing backflips. "Okay," I finally choked out. "Sounds like a plan."

FIVE

"You're fucking *shitting* me?" Arianne screamed into the phone.

I held it out from my ear a second. "I'm as serious as chlamydia," I whispered, once the ringing in my ears had subsided.

"Holy fuck," she muttered, quieter this time, which was good news for my ear drums.

"I know," I agreed.

"Like, *holy fuck*," she repeated.

"I know," I agreed again.

I was in my living room the next morning, still in Hansen's shirt, he was in the shower. I had taken this moment to call my best friend and give her the lowdown of the past twenty-four hours. She obviously knew how I felt about Hansen. About how I had pined for him, while trying not to picture him when the men from the club had me in their bed.

"Geez, who knew, all you needed was a good whack on the

head to stir some masculine sense of protection in that pretty head of his and *bam!* He's yours," she said in amazement.

"Or I'm his," I said, chewing it over in my mind.

"Is there a difference?"

"Oh yes," I told her firmly. "There's a difference.

Arianne was only a visitor in the club world, coming and going as she saw fit. Granted, I was no expert, but I'd spent a lot of time there over the past two years. I saw old ladies come and go. Not frequently, 'go', but a few. A few who didn't understand the life completely didn't understand that in front of the club, they were meant to seem submissive to their men. They were property. In a lot of MCs, I knew this was a bad thing. But with the Sons, it wasn't. It just meant that you needed to re-evaluate how you defined a relationship. And wear the pants behind closed doors.

"Who gives a shit amount semantics babe, just ride the wave. Be happy. You deserve it..." she paused. "Much as I withhold judgment over the life you've lived the past year, hell I've partaken, not to mention my line of work. But, that label, that life of being passed around that wasn't you, babe. You suit the life, don't get me wrong, but not that part of it," she said quietly.

I wasn't offended, but I was surprised. Arianne never pulled punches, and never shied away from telling the truth, whether it was ugly or not. The fact she thought that for two years and didn't say anything, troubled me. Also, the fact that everyone seemed to think I didn't belong in a life I had felt the most like myself in troubled me slightly.

I didn't get the chance to question her on it, on the account of a hot biker that sucked up all the oxygen in my small, but kick-ass living room.

"Gotta go," I said to the phone.

"Hot biker in front of you?" Arianne guessed.

"Yep," I replied, watching him as he stalked toward me.

"Please tell me he's naked," she said. "And if so, find a way to send me a picture."

"Goodbye Arianne," I said as Hansen stopped in front of me.

I hung up and looked up at him. "Arianne says hi."

He grinned and hooked his hands under my arms to lift me up. I automatically wrapped my legs around his waist. I loved that he manhandled me like I weighed nothing. I may have been petite, with small hips and a small ass, but I weighed something. Especially with the boobs God had graced me with.

"You look hot as shit in my tee, still shakin' off sleep, in your fuckin' ridiculous living room," he murmured against my mouth.

"My living room is not ridiculous," I argued. "It's awesome."

Hansen raised a brow, apparently not worried about having this conversation while I was wrapped around his waist. Not that I was complaining.

He looked at my green velvet couch, which had been a great score from a second-hand shop. It had bright pink printed cushions stacked on it, plus a fluffy pink afghan. I had also found a matching armchair, which was beside it. My coffee table was wooden and had a vase of flowers sitting in the middle. I didn't think he was talking about my awesome decorating skills on a budget. I think he may have been referring to my various *Lord Of the Rings* paraphernalia which included figurines scattered around my television, a jewelry stand which had the 'one ring' hanging from a chain, and a framed and signed picture of Viggo Mortensen, AKA Aragon, on the wall. Not to mention my extended DVD set sitting in its rightful place, lording its brilliance over my other, lesser movies.

"You cannot tell me you're not a fan of *Lord of The Rings*, we'd have to break up," I said semi-seriously. I didn't think even the dislike of the three greatest movies of all time would make me want to break up with him. Shit was serious.

Hansen regarded me. "Never seen them."

I opened my mouth in shock. "How is that possible?"

Hansen grinned. "Babe, those movies are three hours long," he stated like this was a problem.

"And?" I probed.

"And, you see me sitting on my ass watching roughly nine hours' worth of anything on television?" he asked.

I chewed my lip. No, I couldn't exactly see Hansen vegging out in front of the television, consuming his body wearing a shirt that said *'What about second breakfast?'* like I did.

"We'll have to change that if we're to remain... whatever we are," I trailed off on labeling us.

Hansen's hands tightened and his nose rubbed against mine. "You're mine, that's what you are," he said firmly. "And if you want me to watch nine hours of anything, you better be prepared to at least give me a blow job while watching it," he joked.

I grinned. "I can do that."

His phone dinged in his pocket. "That'll be Jagger," he said. He kissed me soundly, in a way that made me forget all about Viggo Mortensen, and even the existence of Aragon. And *Legolas*. No easy feat.

"Take it easy. Rest and nothing else," he commanded, depositing me on the couch.

I saluted him. "Yes, sir."

He rolled his eyes and grinned.

"See you, baby," he said softly.

"Bye," I told the rider to his back as he walked out of my house.

I sunk back into my pillows, trying to let the events of the past day and a half sink in. Hansen had driven me home last night, smirked slightly at my house, namely the *LOTR* and *Star Wars* paraphernalia and then got himself a beer, put his feet up on the coffee table and turned on a sports game of some sort. He had, of course, kissed me firmly before this.

I stared at him a moment, in my house, in my space. Relaxed, like he belonged. Then it hit me, he did belong. For however long, he belonged to me. Or like I'd told Arianne, I belonged to him.

Then I'd shaken myself out of it, glued myself to my computer screen and banged out the projects I needed to get done. After giving myself an even bigger headache from being glued to the computer screen, I ordered us some takeout, which we ate in front of the television, then promptly passed out on Hansen's lap. I had awoken when he was carrying me to my room, just in time for him to fuck me senseless.

This morning was the same deal. Although this time, he'd woken me up with his mouth between my legs, suffice to say, it was awesome.

And now I was left alone to process all of this. I didn't exactly know how to process a relationship that had gone from zero to *'you are mine'* in the space of a day. Nor did I want to dwell too much over Hansen's apparent indifference to the fact

I'd slept with his brothers. I wasn't ashamed exactly, I was comfortable with the life I'd chosen, happy with the family it came with and the sex hadn't been bad either. But there was this niggling part of me that wondered if, in the back of his mind, he'd always think of my past as a club whore. Or maybe by some miracle, he wouldn't. Who's to say the men, who I mostly loved and adored wouldn't struggle with this transition. It certainly wasn't normal, not in this chapter anyway.

The fact this had happened so quickly had me searching for the catch. The hidden trick. There had to be one. As much as I wanted this to be what it was, I doubted I'd get exactly what I wanted without some sort of condition.

"STOP FIDGETING," Hansen ordered as we walked into the clubhouse. It was a big concrete structure on the street downtown. It had a sign over the door, 'Sons Of Templar, New Mexico.' The part of town was mostly industrial, and the garage that the boys owned was just down the street. This functioned as sleeping quarters, which were upstairs since the place had three levels. It also had an enormous common area and bar as you walked in, complete with stripper pole and pool table. There was a kitchen and dining area further back and a massive courtyard with picnic tables and fire drums out back. I didn't know what was on the third story. That was strictly members only business.

"I'm not fidgeting," I snapped.

Hansen stopped us just before the doors. He turned me to face him and put his hands lightly on my hips.

"Wanna tell me why you're so nervous?" he asked.

I paused. "I'm yours, right?" I started uncertainly.

Hansen's grip on my hips tightened. "Right," he confirmed firmly.

"Well," I started, looking at my hands. Hansen gripped my chin so I had his eyes.

"Well?"

"Who I've been, what I've been to the club isn't exactly something a man would want his Old Lady to be. The guys might not treat me the same as, Amy, for example."

Hansen's face went hard. "Sometimes I forget, you see the world with your own glasses, babe. Those glasses mostly mean you see goodness and happiness in everyone you met and find a way to joke about even the darkest of shit," he started tightly. "Those glasses obviously also stop you from seeing that, 'cause of who you are. Every single man in there..." he nodded his head to the doors, "...would risk their life, same as they did for Amy. In a heartbeat. Just 'cause of who you were to them doesn't make you any less than her babe..." He paused. "You also should know, every one of those men would've killed to be in my shoes, claim you as their Old Lady. Only thing they're gonna be feeling is stupid for not realizing it sooner. And I'm gonna be feeling proud as shit."

I relaxed slightly at his words, even more at his firm kiss and arm around my shoulders.

We walked into the clubhouse and were greeted with a round of cheers and men raising their bottles. I ignored the glare coming from Kim and was slightly surprised at the small smile from Scar, who was sitting on Charley's knee.

I went slightly red at the attention and was glad when it all died down and we made it to the bar.

Levi came up and slapped Hansen on the shoulder.

"Finally got your head outta your ass I see." He nodded his head to me. "Good thing, I was getting tempted to convince her the perks of being on the back of my bike, if you didn't get your shit together," he said lightly.

I gaped at Levi, and Hansen went slightly stiff. Something seemed to register because he squeezed me tighter and grinned at Levi. "Fuck off," he said lightly.

Levi winked at me then sat down next to us, sipping his beer and shooting the shit, like normal. Only this time, Hansen's arm was firmly wrapped around my chest, pulling me flush to his chest.

It felt kind of weird being in this position when various men came to exchange the odd teasing greeting but otherwise treated us as if we'd been together for longer than say, a day. It also felt nice. Right. Like I'd slipped into a sweater I didn't think would fit, but hugged every inch of me like it had been made for me.

I settled into Hansen's chest, thinking maybe, the other shoe might not drop at all.

A couple of hours and a nice beer buzz later, I made my way to the bathroom, trailing my fingers along the pictures in the hallway. When I was out of view of the common room, I was slammed painfully against those very pictures I'd been tenderly looking at.

Hammer's body pressed against mine, and his alcohol-laden breath permeated my senses.

"Think now your snatch has captured Hansen's attention you can cut off everyone else?" he hissed in my face.

"Step back," I told him firmly, striving to keep the shaking out of my voice. Hammer might be a misogynistic asshole, but he was also a Son. Therefore, he would respect the rules that came with the fact. *Hopefully.*

He ignored me, his hand gripping my hip painfully.

"Once a club whore, always a club whore," he shot cruelly.

"Step back, Hammer," I repeated.

Again, he ignored me. "I don't think Hansen's gonna want tainted goods, once he realizes every man in this club's had a taste of that pussy," he continued, his words hitting their mark.

That's it. I was done. I may be small, but I didn't lie to Hansen. Living the life I'd lived, in the neighborhood I'd lived it, I knew how to take care of myself. Which was why I brought my knee up to his crotch. *Hard.*

He cried out and stumbled back, gripping between his legs.

"Bitch," he shouted his eyes slits.

"What's going on here?" a deep and pissed off voice asked.

I moved my eyes to land on Grim, the club president and all around scary mofo. He was old, his hair more salt than pepper, his tanned face showing more than a few lines as evidence of his age. He wore it well and was still in pretty good shape, his tattoo-covered arms were also defined with muscle. He had an Old Lady, who he was faithful to, which meant I'd never really been in his immediate presence. He also scared the shit out of me. He hardly ever cracked a smile and always looked ready to knife someone, hence the road name.

"Bitch fuckin' kneed me in the balls," Hammer told him, glaring at me.

"Snitch," I hissed.

I could be in serious shit here. A woman, a relative second class citizen in this world could not lay their hands on a patched member. As I well knew.

Grim's eyes settled on me. "Macy, with me," he ordered briskly, walking past me and in the direction of the door titled 'Church.'

Hammer grinned at me evilly and I followed on wooden legs.

Church was a place no woman was allowed and somewhere where I guessed I would be getting banished from my family. My heart sank. Not even a week of living my dream and it'd already shot it to shit.

Classic Macy.

I was mentally thinking about how I'd bury myself in my fantasy world of Middle Earth to try and escape the pain of being exiled from the only family I'd had since I lost my own.

"Shut the door behind you and sit down," Grim commanded.

I silently complied, sitting down in front of him. I met his eyes. I didn't offer an explanation, or excuses. Hammer was in the wrong, but I wasn't going to even bother telling Grim that. His loyalty would be with his brother, not some club whore turned Old Lady. Hammer's treatment of me showed I was unlikely to be considered a true Old Lady.

He regarded me levelly. "Been with Linda almost fifteen years," he declared, taking me totally off guard. He didn't address my no doubt wide eyes. "Longer than most of the boys in this chapter have been around," he continued, clasping his hands together. "Which means, save a couple of lifers, no one knows Linda used to hold a position in the club very different than the President's Old Lady," he told me.

I got what he was alluding to. And it knocked my preverbal socks right off. Linda was the quintessential biker queen. Even pushing fifty, she was a beauty, albeit slightly hard. Every single one of the men treated her like the matriarch she was. Though she could be equally as scary as Grim, she'd always treated most of the club girls with respect. Well, apart from Kim, but she was a total bitch, who tried her best to flirt with Grim when no one was looking. She was kind of my hero. The woman I had always wanted to be.

"Found it difficult, she did, transitioning from who she was to Old Lady," he continued. "Thought I'd have a problem with it. I didn't," he told me firmly. "Didn't give a shit who came before me, long as no one came after me. Brothers accepted it readily. Bitch was born to be an Old Lady. She had to find that out for herself, though. Decide if the club, the way we lived, was for her. That was her way of finding out." Grim's clear gray eyes didn't leave mine. "No one thought any less of her. I sure as shit didn't. Long as she was loyal to me, loved me, loved the club, other shit meant nothing. You'd do well to remember that," Grim finished.

I sat back, digesting the story. "So you're not sending me away?" I whispered.

Grim frowned. "No, I'm not," he said firmly.

My entire body relaxed. "Thank you," I told him quietly.

Grim stood, making his way over to me. "Don't need to thank me. We got rules here. Hammer spat in the face of those rules, he'll be dealt with," he told me tightly. "Gonna ask you to keep this chat between us. Same as *that* incident." He nodded his head to the hallway. "Don't think Hammer's gonna be too eager to share a tiny bitch almost sterilized him." He looked like he might almost smile and I think his voice might have held respect. I was shocked.

"Also, I think Hansen might finish the job if he finds out.

Don't want shit going down in my club over pussy, even an Old Lady. Which is what you are now," he continued.

I nodded by answer.

"Go back to the party, enjoy the time with your old man. Don't let a drunken idiot's words get into your head," he ordered.

I got up and surprised the shit out of myself by kissing Grim on his tanned cheek and then darting from the room before he forgot that he was meant to be a big bad motorcycle club President and not a caring, wise man giving relationship advice.

Luckily, I didn't see Hammer on the way back to the party and happily went back to Hansen's arms, letting him kiss me soundly in front of the crowd.

What I didn't do, was let go of those words. Instead, I let them settle deep down in my gut, tainting the feeling of warmth that had originally been pure and happy.

SIX

"You get dressed in the dark today girl? You seem to have forgotten your pants," my grandmother commented as I met her in the common room of her facility.

It was as cheerful as a place like that could be, with dated old sofas and an ancient television playing some random game show. Various older people were scattered around, some looking well dressed and relatively stable, others wearing tattered robes and muttering to themselves. The saddest, I thought, was an old woman in fuzzy slippers staring vacantly out the window. Every time I came here, she was sitting in that same spot, staring into the distance.

"What can I say, Grandma, not all of us can have the time-less sense of style you have," I replied.

My empire line printed dress stopped above my knees and had bell sleeves. My tan over the knee boots meant only a smallish square of skin was showing. I thought I looked awesome, as did Hansen, who showed me his complete appreciation for my boots only hours before. My grandmother did not obviously agree with a self-confessed style savant and a smokin' hot biker, who seemed to have taken permanent residence in my mind. And maybe my heart.

She shook her head in disapproval. "You'd think I'd taught you nothing," she snapped.

Not true. She taught me a life of bitterness and negativity may not wither the looks, but it did land you in an old folks' home with a dementia diagnosis. Not that I'd say anyone deserved that, but I thought maybe karma might have played a part in this one.

"You still wasting time playing on computers instead of having a real job?" She moved from my outfit to my occupation in a not so smooth segway.

"I'm a graphic designer Grandma, it doesn't exactly consist of playing on computers," I explained like I had countless times. It didn't matter I was actually good at my job and earned a decent amount of money. Money that helped pay for what the insurance didn't cover for this place.

She waved her hand. "Don't want to hear excuses as to why you won't get a real job. I'm assuming this has to do with the company you keep. *Bikers*," she spat the word in distaste.

You'd think, with her haughty attitude, my grandmother was an upper-middle-class lady who had never encountered people like the 'thugs' I spent my time with. Therefore, giving some reason as why she brought into the stereotype.

That was not the case.

She raised me, after my parents died, in what could loosely be described as the ghetto. Or at least on the edge of the ghetto.

Our house was tiny and well-kept with an immaculate garden and a sofa which still had the plastic on, but I regularly walked past drug deals and gangbangers on my way to and from school. My grandmother, who'd been living on a pension and the benefit from the state when she got me, had some sort of selective vision. That stuff did not exist for her. She lived on a high horse, where she had a prime view of all of my shortcomings, of which there were many. She still put a roof over my head, and food in my belly—when she decided I wasn't 'pudgy'—and she was my mother's mother, so she deserved some degree of respect. Despite the fact she was a raving shrew.

My silence didn't mean she'd stopped her tirade about how she was going to die early because her granddaughter caused her heart to break from disappointment. I smoothly changed the subject and moved her onto complaining about the staff and the food instead of my life, which she found lacking.

MY WHOLE BODY relaxed when I stepped out of the doors once more.

"Survived another visit I see?" a familiar voice asked.

I looked to my side to see Robert, this time wearing a cable knit jumper that looked seriously expensive, and jeans that looked like he'd bought them faded. Instead of wearing them like that, like bikers I knew.

"Do I have scratch marks on my face? Or are they invisible to the human eye?" I asked seriously.

He laughed and stepped forward. "Looks beautiful to me. Although, I know whatever you endure in there is not outwardly apparent," he stated lightly, though his eyes held something that told me humor was the only way to deal with the reality of that terrible place.

I ignored the *'beautiful'* comment, it made my slightly uncomfortable.

"Who have you got in there?" I nodded my head. "If you don't mind me asking," I added quickly, not knowing the etiquette for this particular social situation. Even in situations I did theoretically know the etiquette, I always managed to put a foot in my mouth.

"My mom, and I don't mind you asking. It's nice to talk to someone who knows, although I know my mom wouldn't metaphorically rip me to shreds if she knew who I was. She was more likely to worry that I wasn't getting enough sleep," he said quietly.

"Your mom?" I asked softly. This man couldn't have been much older than me, definitely not old enough to have a senile mother.

He looked at me with pain in his eyes. "Early onset Alzheimers," he explained.

Out of reflex, I touched his arm lightly. "I'm sorry," I told him genuinely. "I don't have a mom, so I can't imagine how hard it would be having her right here but losing her none-theless."

He smiled sadly at me. "That's exactly what it feels like. It's why I stand here a few minutes before I go in. To mentally prepare myself to visit my mom's body. And to catch a glimpse of a pretty girl," he added with a small smile.

I smiled back. Again, I thought about what a genuinely nice guy he was. Too bad I was currently infatuated with a biker. Even if I wasn't, I wasn't the kind of girl a man like that would end up with.

"But, you're spoken for," he continued. "That still the case?"

I nodded. Yes, this time I was spoken for, in the traditional sense, by one man instead of an entire motorcycle club.

"Thought so," he said. He fished into his pocket to retrieve a card out of his wallet. He handed it to me. "That ever changes, or you just need to talk... use that." He nodded at the card.

"Robert Frank, Attorney," I read and raised a brow. "Very grown up and serious," I commented.

I thought about what Hansen's business card would say, *'Hansen—Biker, Hot Guy and all around Badass.'* I furrowed my brows when I realized I didn't strictly know what he did to afford his small but impressive house, or to feed his muscled body with the protein it needed.

Robert misconstrued my frown. "Don't hold the lawyer thing against me, I do my best to hide my scales beneath suits," he joked.

I laughed, despite myself. My face turned serious. "I'm sorry about your mom," I said sadly, squeezing his arm again.

He gave me a long look. "I'm sorry about your grandmother," he said sincerely before moving to walk through the doors.

I watched him walk away for a second, feeling profoundly sad for Robert the lawyer and nice guy, and his mother.

THE PAST TWO weeks had been nothing short of amazing. Hansen and I had spent almost every night together. Mostly at his place, because of his attitude toward my neighborhood, and the fact his house was way better than mine. I liked the quiet. The lack of sirens and gunshots was calming. And the fact it was Hansen's. And I was there. And he treated me like it was going to be a permanent thing. He even told me to put my 'girly shit' in a drawer in the bathroom. Then I had commenced a freak-out, called Arianne, then went and bought 'girly shit' to put in my newly acquired drawer.

We spent little time at the club, and I was glad of the fact. The transition from what I was to Old Lady was proving more difficult than I thought. Most of the other girls joked with me apart from a couple that gave me the stink eye, which I ignored. Still, being an Old Lady meant I wasn't required to run after the other members, that I should theoretically, treat the other girls like I was somehow superior. Which I would never do. They weren't better or worse than me. That would never change. Linda had even seemed to accept me into the fold, sharing a beer with me and chatting like we were old friends. I tried not to put my foot in my mouth the entire time. The fact I didn't have a spike heeled boot embedded in said foot told me I'd succeeded.

Hansen treated me as if he hadn't almost ignored me for the past year like he'd been with me longer than two weeks. Like I was where I was meant to be. The sex—sweet mother, the sex—was better than I'd ever imagined. It was something more than his talents in the bedroom, which were substantial, it was the connection we had, the intangible, unspoken something between us that brought so much more depth to it.

It was after one of these amazing love making sessions that I decided it was time to burst the bubble. Start living in the real world. I rested my elbow on his chest and put my head in my hands.

"Why no girls?" I asked him abruptly.

Hansen was used to me blurting things out without much warning or forethought, but his raised eyebrow showed he needed more information.

"Since you arrived from the Nevada chapter, there's been no girls," I clarified. "None from the club anyway, why?" I expanded.

Hansen looked at me for a long while. "I wasn't celibate if that's what you're alluding," he said carefully.

I nodded. "Didn't think so. A man who had been battling blue balls for the better part of a year wouldn't have lasted as long as you did with me the first time," I said firmly.

Hansen chuckled slightly.

I forged on. "So why not girls from the club?" I asked, not really knowing if I wanted the answer.

Hansen regarded me. "'Cause, if I were going to fuck any bitch who was a regular at the club, it would've been a pixie-haired half pint with beautiful eyes and a smart mouth, no one else," he said finally. "Subconsciously, part of me seemed to know I was gonna claim you at some point. When I did that, I didn't want you to have to deal with those vipers."

I opened my mouth shock. "You're shitting me?" I asked ungracefully.

He smirked. "I'm not shitting you, babe. Other bitches at the club might've been easy on the eyes, but they weren't you. Didn't fuck you because I knew if I got a taste, I wouldn't be able to let you go, I'd trap you in this life. When I realized you're in it for good, that's when I realized I needed to get my shit together... claim you. Night at the bar gave me the push I needed."

"Don't put me up on a pedestal," I pleaded. "It'll only hurt when I hurtle down off it. When you realize I'm not some delicate flower that naïvely walked into a biker den to get her soul corrupted," I told him. I was far from naïve when I walked in. I'd known exactly what I was getting myself into.

His face turned hard, but I continued.

"My life isn't daisies and butterflies. My life is far from innocent or good. My parents were murdered when I was twelve. I saw them die, watched them bleed out," I told him and his body jerked. "I was sent to live with my only living relative, one who my mother didn't even speak to. One who was meaner than half the gang bangers on the streets she lived on," I told him honestly. "I went from a home full of love to a house which seeped hatred. Bitterness. I lived that, breathed that, for six years..." I paused. "I wasn't always a happy person. My parents' death, my fork-tongued grandmother, they created an angry, troubled teenager. One that tried to find love in various boys. Some were nice, others weren't..." I trailed off and watched Hansen's jaw harden exponentially.

I wasn't going to elaborate on my years thinking sex equaled love. Nor was I going to educate him on how I found out the hard way, after one of the boys that 'loved' me smacked me around. A swift punch in the face and a couple of broken ribs taught me the truth.

"I was always searching for something, searching for the family I'd lost," I explained, moving my thoughts away from my troubled teen years. "Didn't have it with my own blood, I escaped at eighteen, had nothing but the clothes on my back and a few hundred bucks to secure me a room in a dingy motel.

Did crap at school, apart from with computers. I loved them, was good with them. But I couldn't afford one, had no other discernable skills or qualifications, so I stripped." I tried for nonchalance, not looking at Hansen, afraid of the judgment I'd find behind his eyes. I couldn't handle that, so I traced the scar on his chest.

"I'm not ashamed of it," I declared. "Of the fact I stripped for a year. I met Arianne, made enough money to take care of myself, I survived. Somehow, during that time, I realized the difference between a good life and a bad life was attitude. If I held onto that anger that I had at the world for the shitty hand I was dealt, it'd turn me into an angry and bitter person. It'd turn me into my grandma." I shivered at the thought. "So I let it go. All of it. Saved my money, got enough to get a computer, started bringing in clients and making enough money to quit stripping." I shrugged. "And the rest, as they say, is history." I chewed my lip. "Then I found the club. Saw what it was. A dysfunctional, rowdy, and rough around the corners family. Somewhere I could belong."

I finished my little speech, finally meeting his eyes. They didn't betray anything, but his hands tightened around my body. "That's why I need you to see *me*," I whispered. "See who I am as an imperfect person. One who isn't some imagined version of who you think I am. Someone who deserves *something better*. I was a stripper, a club whore, and now I'm your Old Lady. This for me *is better*. The best," I told him truthfully. "Who I am, what I've gone through... I'm not set for the traditional life. The one where you're expected to fit within some sort of predestined mold. Where they make you color neatly between the lines. I've never been able to stick inside the lines. I want to be free to go outside them, color my own life."

I pursed my lips. Though I talked a lot, all the time actually, that was the most I'd actually *said* to anyone, *ever*.

Hansen searched my face for a long while, then he flipped me on my back, framing my face with his hands. "First, you don't call yourself a club whore again. *Ever*. That's not what you were. Not how I think of you. You were someone wading through a shitty life, trying to find their way," he said firmly. "Every word you've just said, makes me believe you're even more perfect than I'd imagined. You're perfect because of your imperfections, 'cause of the life you've survived. You've fought your way through and still found a way to be this..." he stroked my jaw, "...this beautiful, funny, goofy woman who carries the world on her shoulders, but fuckin' skips through life like nothing weighs her down. The one who has the sweetest pussy I've ever tasted, the kindest heart I've ever witnessed. You make me determined to give you everything you want. Everything you deserve," he declared.

A lone tear seeped out of the corner of my eye at his words.

His mouth hovered over mine. He wiped the tear off my face with his thumb gently. "And baby, you do fit in a mold. One I didn't even know I'd created. One that was made for the woman who I would want to be on the back of my bike, warm my bed, own my soul," he growled, claiming my mouth before I could do anything stupid, like propose.

He kissed me with a ferocity that healed all the wounds I'd exposed to him. That filled me up so completely after the beauty of his words. He ran his hands down my hips, cocking my leg so it wrapped around me.

"You ever take anyone raw, babe?" he asked tightly, poised at my entrance.

I shook my head, unable to speak.

"Neither have I, never. Told myself the only one I'd take with nothing in between us, would be the woman who I intended to keep in my bed forever," he whispered, roughly, plunging into me on his last word.

I cried out, his words, his beautiful, heart-warming words, along with the intensity of his intrusion overwhelmed me.

He took me, hard but slow, every stroke a promise, a vow. His mouth lightly brushed mine while his eyes seemed to capture my soul and brand it with his claim.

"I love you," I whispered, unable to hold it in. I needed to say it, in this beautiful moment, had to complete it.

His body froze, he hovered over my mouth. "Think I loved you the first moment I saw you, babe. Realized it the moment you called me honey at four in the morning outside the club-house," he told me thrusting into me once more.

His mouth captured mine, muffling the sounds of my climax. I felt him empty himself inside me, as I milked his release out of me. He stayed on top of me, inside me, watching me. Saying everything and nothing at the same time. I winced slightly at the emptiness as he gently pulled out of me. He kissed my nose.

"Be right back," he promised.

I watched his muscled back walk through to his ensuite, taking a moment to appreciate the firm and tight ass that I could totally stare at for days. That man, with the great ass and great everything else. That man loved me. *Me*. The real me and his love was a promise of the life I'd always hoped for.

He returned and gently cleaned me with a washcloth, the

intimacy and tenderness of the moment jarring me. With that taken care of, he gathered me in his arms. We lay quietly, for once I was content with silence. I'd said enough tonight.

"Your grandmother," Hansen said finally, his voice hard. "She's the one you visit every Saturday?"

I nodded. He knew I visited a relative every Saturday, as I had for the past two weeks we'd been together, but since I hadn't told him the whole gory story until before, I didn't really elaborate. Jagger and Arianne were the only ones who knew about her.

"Why?" he asked. "I imagine that bitch doesn't appreciate nor deserve those visits, nor do I miss the fact your smile's slightly dimmer after them. So why?"

Nothing got past him. He had silently watched me the past two Saturdays. It took me a while to shake off the insults, the barbs that accumulate in one hour's visit. So I wasn't surprised he noticed.

I shrugged. "She's got no one else. She's my only family at the end of the day, and she's the last connection I've got with my mom. I just feel that I should, you know? That I'd be a bad person if I didn't," I added.

Hansen paused. "You've got a family, babe," he said finally. "One you've chosen, one who's got your back no matter what. Blood doesn't mean shit when that connection turns rancid. Blood is what ties you together when there's nothing else, nothing good left. The club, that's stronger than that, because that's the family you choose, the one where you belong," he told me. "You're not a bad person, shit babe, enduring the shit she put you through and still going to visit the old bat? They should consider you for sainthood." His voice was slightly teasing but there was something more serious was underneath.

"I don't want you going 'cause anything that dims that beautiful smile is something I want to get you away from... protect you from. It's your choice, though, babe. I'll be here, no matter what."

I smiled at him and I smiled on the inside. No, beamed. Every part of me.

SEVEN

"I'm not moving in," I declared firmly.

Hansen's face hardened. "Why the fuck not?"

I held my hands out, splattering spaghetti sauce unwillingly as I did so. Some landed on the wall, luckily Hansen's eyes were on me and not on the fact I was ruining the furniture. I decided to act natural. Natural equaled slightly pissed at this moment. "Um, because it's way too fast. The standard rules of dating constitute at least six months go by before we even *consider* cohabitation," I informed him, moving my attention back to the dinner I was cooking. Or maybe ruining. I lived on takeout and peanut butter usually. I was going for domestic goddess but I was hurtling toward domestic fuckup.

It was almost a week after the exchange of the I love you's. I'd been floating on a cloud since then. I didn't give a fuck how cheesy that sounded, I was. Well, until Hansen had declared, yes *declared*, I was moving in.

"Clue in babe, we're nothing close to normal," he clipped moving to stand beside me. His hand moved to jerk my chin toward him. "You said yourself, you don't color between the lines. Why do you give a fuck about what we're supposed to do? Do what you want to do. I want you in my house. Want you to make it ours. Want to see your stupid elf shit on the walls, have your girly cushions on my sofa. I want you," he said fiercely.

"You've got me," I whispered.

He searched my eyes. "Well, move the fuck in," he ordered.

"Okay," I said automatically. *Shit.* I didn't even mean to agree. He hypnotized me. Used *LOTR* against me.

He let go of my chin. "Good," he muttered, before moving to answer his cell phone which had cut off my belated protests.

"What," he greeted. Yes, he answered his phone with the word '*what*'—men.

He frowned and moved out of earshot, clipping answers into the phone.

I watched while I stirred my sauce. I was yet to ask any further questions about his role in the club, about the club in general. I knew the bare minimum that they owned the garage downtown, they fixed cars and bikes. I also knew they did a lot more than that. They did things that had got them raided twice in the past year. Granted, the cops didn't find anything, but I didn't think they went around raiding people for shits and giggles. I was under no illusions, they were a one percenter gang. They worked on the wrong side of the law most of the time. Lived by their own rules. I didn't exactly agree with it, but I got it. I didn't have any high hopes about the club turning legit like I'd heard the Cali chapter was moving toward. I fell in love with Hansen, with the club warts and all, I'd continue to love them. That's how family worked.

I just didn't know if I could handle being in the dark. Having to understand 'club business' served as an explanation, or as an excuse.

Hansen walked back to me, his face hard. "This shit is reheatable, right?" He nodded to the sauce.

I nodded.

"Okay, I'll have it later. Got to go, club business. Go do shit with Arianne, or the girls," he said. "Don't wait up. Want you to go to bed naked," he ordered.

He kissed me soundly, squeezed my ass, then left. I stood in the same spot and heard his Harley rumble away.

The cold reality of my life as an Old Lady began to sink in. I had a feeling I would have to cook a lot of reheatable dinners in the near future. I couldn't find it in myself to get pissed. It was part of the life. Part that I'd have to live with. A part I'd live with happily if it meant a life with Hansen.

So I finished cooking dinner, ate some, wrapped up the rest and settled in at my computer. I toyed with the idea of calling Arianne, but I was happy to have a night of solitude to escape into my computer, and get a head start on some projects.

My phone ringing an hour or so later jerked me out of the trance I got into whenever I lost myself in my work.

"Macy?" a familiar voice greeted once I answered.

A familiar voice that made my stomach drop. "Please tell me you're calling to catch up and tell me you've decided to name your first born Macy," I said weakly.

"Sorry sweetheart," Jim said in a hushed tone. "I wanted you to hear it from me..." he paused, I knew what was coming before he even said it. "He got parole."

My breath left me in a whoosh and a thousand little

pinpricks pierced my body. "I don't..." I took a breath, "...I don't get how that happened. He got life. He took two lives. That should mean *life*," I said fiercely. A hatred that I didn't even know I was capable of bubbled up inside me.

I heard Jim sigh into the phone. "Yeah, girl, if there was such a thing as justice, they would've fried him the day I arrested him," he said with fury.

I struggled to get my heart from beating out of my chest. "So he's going to be free," I said finally. "The man who shot my parents in cold blood is going to walk around breathing the same air as me after twelve years," I said flatly.

"I'm so sorry, sweetheart," Jim spoke softly.

I jerked out of my cold rage. "It's not your fault, Jim. Thanks for calling." I mustered up some warmth for the cop who still called every year on my parents' anniversary.

"We'll meet for coffee tomorrow," he said firmly. He was a good guy. A good cop. Too bad that meant shit in this crappy world.

"Yeah," I said weakly.

I hung up the phone. Feeling everything—pain, anger, hurt. Anger—*that was it*. No—*fury*. I couldn't swallow it, couldn't let it go. It seemed to consume me.

I needed numbness.

———

"YOUR PHONE'S ringing for the millionth time," Arianne slurred.

I squinted at it. Hansen's name came up on the screen. I ignored it as I had the other five calls. I couldn't deal with him. Couldn't deal with myself. I needed my best friend and a bottle of vodka. I just needed numbness and Hansen made me feel. I couldn't feel right now.

"You should answer that," she said, pointing at the now silent phone. "He'll get all..." she waved her hands dramatically, "...psycho biker."

I inspected her reasoning. Yes, most likely Hansen would get all psycho biker, considering I'd left his house and driven straight to Arianne's, where we'd almost demolished a bottle of vodka and I had embraced the numbness.

My phone dinged. Another text.

HANSEN: *Macy. Answer your fucking phone. Tell me where you are.*

"HE COULD PROBABLY HAVE him whacked you know," Arianne informed me, making me look up from my phone. "You tell him and..." she made a finger gun with her hand and pointed it at her head, "...scumbag *down.*"

I shook away the bitterness that came with that thought. "I'm not asking my boyfriend to whack someone," I slurred.

Arianne's eyes narrowed. "This isn't a *someone.* He's not a person, the man that did this. He's an animal. Plus, you tell Hansen, you probably wouldn't even have to ask," she commented.

My phone dinged.

HANSEN: *Macy. I'm getting seriously concerned. Where the fuck are you?*

. . .

ARIANNE'S WORDS RESONATED. Because I feared they
were true. The world I'd found myself in was a world of
loyalty and love. With that loyalty came the need for revenge
on anyone who hurt the club. With that love came brutality.

I typed into the phone.

ME: *Need numbness. You make me feel. I'm okay. Safe. Just
need to be numb for the night.*

I READ over my text with drunken eyes, deduced it made
sense, then switched off my phone. Arianne watched me. She
didn't say a word, didn't judge, just passed me the vodka bottle.

Man, I loved her.

———

I WOKE to loud banging which seemed to shake Arianne's
tiny apartment. I squinted and deduced it was coming from
the door.

"Open the fuckin' door," a voice bellowed.

A very angry voice.

A very angry familiar voice.

I detached my hand from Arianne's who was yet to wake
up and half rolled, half fell off the sofa.

"Ouch," I muttered as my head hit the corner of the coffee
table. It didn't exactly hurt, but I thought such impact was
meant to cause pain, so I uttered to appropriate word.

Okay, still numb, which meant still drunk. I pulled myself to my feet and fought against the swaying floor to make it to the door. *Definitely still drunk.* That and the fact it was still dark must have meant it was still night-time.

After battling with the chain, I was blinded by horrible, bright sunlight when I opened the door. I put my hand up to shade myself. *Okay, not night.* Arianne just had really great curtains.

"Jesus fuckin' Christ," I heard an angry voice mutter.

I squinted to see Hansen taking up the doorway. His entire frame seemed to be etched in fury.

"What time is it?" I asked, wondering how it was so bright and how I was still resonantly drunk.

There was a pause. "What time is it?" Hansen repeated in a dangerously quiet voice. One which I should have registered as a warning.

I was drunk and disorientated so I didn't. So, instead, I nodded.

Note to self, don't nod. It hurts head.

"You're fucking serious?" he yelled. "I come home, you've disappeared, no note, no call, you're fuckin' computer's still open. You don't answer your phone, not for hours, then you send some fucked up text and turn off your phone. Now, I finally find you, after driving myself fuckin' crazy with worry all night, and you ask me what time it is?" he bellowed.

I flinched, not only at his anger but at the fact the volume of his voice was very painful to my fast approaching hangover.

He seemed to take my flinch as fear, so he took a deep breath and seemed to make an effort to calm himself. "What the fuck, Macy?" he said quieter, but no less angry. "You can't do shit like that, just take off. Is this about me asking you to move in? You got a problem, you talk, you don't fuckin take off without a word," his voice began to rise again.

I squinted at him, and swayed slightly, unable to properly comprehend so much while dealing with the transition between drunk to hungover.

Hansen steadied me by clutching my hips. "You're drunk?" he said in disbelief.

I nodded. "Seems that way."

"It's nine a.m.," he pointed out through gritted teeth.

I tilted my head. "Well, that vodka was certainly worth every penny," I mused out loud.

"So you put me through all this shit..." he returned to that dangerous quiet voice, "...to tie one on?"

He didn't even wait for me to answer, just let go of my hips and stepped back. "Got shit to do," he clipped, his voice tight. "You wanna talk about whatever the fuck this is..." he gestured to my body, "...you do it when you've sobered up."

He didn't even wait for a response, just sauntered off and left me standing there, squinting into the harsh morning sunlight. Then they came the feelings. So, I stumbled back into Arianne's kitchen, poured myself a glass of orange juice and splashed a liberal amount of vodka into it.

"My kind of mimosas," Arianne commented, slightly slurring her words. She grabbed my glass stole a sip, then sank back on the sofa. "Make me one if you're morning drinking, I can't let you do it alone," she declared.

Totally loved her.

"Honey, I love a bender as much as the next girl, and I totally get why you're drowning your sorrows. How about we transition to coffee?" Arianne suggested after two glasses, and an hour later.

I thought on it.

Coffee. Coffee meant sober. Sober meant hangover. Hangovers came with regrets, and the stern reality of life prior to drunkenness. I wanted to stay in a perpetual state of drunkenness to avoid the reality that I knew was coming. I knew that was strictly labeled as alcoholism, and I didn't want that. I also wanted to prolong my holiday from reality—from pain.

"Or," Arianne said, on my pause. "We could get showered, put on awesome bathing suits and hit this pool party I was invited to?" she suggested.

I grinned. "You totally get me," I told her.

She cupped my face. "I totally get the need you have to finally uncoil and feel all that pain that's been building up for years. This might not be the most sensible way to do it. But fuck sensible, we may as well have some fun while we're drowning our sorrows," she said with a sad smile.

THE MUSIC WAS LOUD. Too loud to hear what the tool beside me was saying, thank God. He'd taken it upon himself to fill the empty sun lounger beside me. Since I'd left Arianne on the dance floor and decided to pass out in the sun, this guy had taken my solitude as in invitation to hit on me. I tried my hardest to nicely reject him, but he wasn't taking the hint. I decided to go straight to ignoring him. Plus, he couldn't see my eyes were shut under my shades.

After a few minutes, he seemed to go silent and I was glad for him finally going away. Then, I felt a shadow mask the rays of the sun, therefore hindering my tan.

"Dude, down in front," I said with closed eyes, hoping he could hear me over the music.

The shadow remained, so I guessed not. I opened my eyes to see the shadow was not dressed in swim trunks, nor looking like he was having any fun. This shadow was wearing all black and had a familiar leather cut over the top of his black tee. His eyes were hidden by my dark shades, but the hardness of his jaw told me he was pissed. I noticed Jagger and Charley were behind him. Jagger looked slightly less pissed and a little more concerned. Charley was checking out the tits of some girl walking past him.

I pushed my shades on top of my head, just in time for Hansen to roughly grab my arm and yank me up.

He reached down and snatched my cover-up from beside me. "Put that on. Now," he clipped in my ear.

I complied, because even in my drunkenness, I could see the danger in his eyes. My eyes landed on Arianne, who was now standing with Jagger, his hand circling her wrist. She shrugged her shoulders and grinned. Crazy bitch.

After I had yanked my floaty kaftan over my head, Hansen grabbed my arm and proceeded to drag me through the throngs of people and out through the fancy hallway of whoever's mansion it was we were attending the party.

"Hansen," I started as he stopped me in front of an SUV.

He turned his head from the door, which he was opening for me. "Not a fuckin' word," he clipped, his voice colder than I'd ever heard it. "Get in the fuckin' car, Macy," he ordered.

I complied, again, out of self-preservation.

He rounded the car and screeched out of the driveway in silence. I fiddled with the tassels on my kaftan. I had switched to water not long ago but was still feeling pretty buzzed.

"You eaten today?" he said finally, his voice tightened.

"Do strawberry daiquiris count?" I asked.

Hansen's eyes cut to me. "What the fuck do you think?"

"Well, I'm not sure of their actual ingredients, but since they taste remarkably like strawberries I'm guessing maybe… since fruit counts as food," I rambled.

My eyes landed on Hansen. I was guessing he was expecting a no. He didn't say anything more, just directed us to a drive through and promptly ordered.

"Eat," he commanded, thrusting the greasy bag at me.

Suddenly, I was ravenous and inhaled the burger and fries that it contained.

Once I'd finished, I realized the air in the cab was humming. That may be because the food had done its job to soak up the alcohol swirling around in my stomach.

"You're mad," I observed.

Hansen's hands tightened on the steering wheel. I noticed his knuckles were turning white.

"Mad, was about six hours ago, right after I realized you were whole and safe. After finding you half naked, half wasted, sprawled on a sun lounger while greasy fuckers glared at you, I'm fuckin' *furious*," he muttered.

With his presence and the grim reality of soberness, came pain. Came the truth. The bitter, ugly truth that I was trying to escape.

"I can explain," I started in a weak voice.

"Don't wanna hear it," he cut me off. "We'll talk when you've slept it off. When you're not coasting off a fuckin' two-day bender," he clipped in disgust.

I flinched at his tone and turned my head. I was thankful,

not for his anger but for the respite. At least now I could keep running for a little longer.

I AWOKE DYING. Or at the very least suffering from some horrible brain-eating virus. I thought a moment.

Nope, just hungover.

Very hungover. I squeezed my eyes shut, willing my body to lapse back into unconsciousness until I was able to physically handle the pain. It didn't work. I lay very still, trying to get my bearings and handle the pain I put myself through.

I opened my eyes and saw I was in a familiar room. Hansen's room. Events came rushing back. That night at Arianne's—ignoring his calls. The next morning—how angry he was. Then my brilliant decision to go to a pool party and continue drinking. Instead of sober up and explain myself to Hansen. I couldn't even remember getting to bed, let alone getting changed into the tee I was wearing.

There was a glass of water and two aspirin beside the bed. *He couldn't hate me that much.* I sucked down the water and swallowed the aspirin.

"Always helped mom," a quiet voice declared.

I jumped, which wasn't the best idea for my delicate head. Hansen sat in the corner, on an old armchair, his elbows resting on his knees.

"What?" I croaked, confused, and slightly hurt at the empty look in his eyes.

He nodded to the glass. "Two aspirin and water... helped her shake off the worst of it. Usually, so she could stomach her morning drink," he clarified. "Learned that at ten years old, to put those there," he continued. "That was, of course, after I dragged her to bed."

His heartbreaking words began to sink in. "Your mom was—"

"An alcoholic," he finished bitterly. "Yep. Most of my memories of her were when she had a drink in her hand, or when she was passed out clutching the bottle," he explained without emotion.

It all sunk in. Hansen was always at the bar, or sitting at the club. He watched, joked with his brothers, stared at me, but he never drank. Might have a beer every now and then, but never more than two.

"Hansen—" I tried to speak, sitting up.

"Died when I was seventeen," he cut me off again. "Plowed her car into a power pole. Lucky it was only herself she killed, not some innocent family. Lucky I turned eighteen the next day, so I didn't end up in the system. So I could enlist," he carried on.

My heart hurt—no *bled*—with his words.

"Don't begrudge you, you want to let loose... have beers... have fun," he continued. "But when you decide to take off with no word, have me picturing your lifeless body in a ditch somewhere, only to find you sprawled at some McMansion in a getup that barely covers your pussy? That shit is not fucking okay," he said quietly. Just because he didn't yell didn't mean I didn't feel the depth of his anger.

I pushed off the bed shakily and made my way over to him. His jaw was hard as he watched me approach.

"I can explain," I whispered, standing in front of him, not sure if I should touch.

"Yeah, so could she. Don't have time to listen to excuses

now, babe. Should've been at the club an hour ago. Been waiting for you to wake up. Make sure you were okay with my own two eyes," he said coldly, standing up.

We stood close, but not touching. My eyes prickled because our proximity didn't change the fact I felt miles away from him.

"Now I've seen that I've got to roll. We'll talk, figure this shit out. Maybe when I'm a little less fuckin' furious." He touched my cheek briefly, but didn't say a word and then turned to leave.

I watched woodenly as he disappeared down the corner of the hallway. I then crawled back into his bed and stared at the ceiling. His indifference, his anger, was well founded. But, I also didn't know that shit about his mom. If I did, I would've done things differently. He also was supposed to know me, know that I didn't do shit like yesterday on a whim. He should know that I wouldn't leave like I did without a reason. He couldn't see past *his* anger, couldn't even give me the time to explain. Not when club business was waiting.

I rolled over and groaned when I realized the day. Saturday. Visit with the she-devil day. And I had to do it hungover. The universe freaking loved me. Little did I know the universe had far from finished with me.

EIGHT

I have no idea how I did it. Survived an hour with grandma feeling like death warmed up and nursing a snit with my boyfriend. And battling the debilitating fury that had settled at the base of my stomach knowing *he* was out there. Free to live his life. Finished the measly sentence, while I would never escape my lifetime sentence. But I did. I let the insults about my hair, my job, the fact I looked like a drug addict today, I let all of it slide over me.

But when I got out, I struggled to get it under control. Get myself breathing right.

"Macy?" a concerned voice asked from beside me.

I glanced to see Robert push off from the wall he was leaning on to approach me, his worried eyes taking me in.

I sucked in a breath and straightened.

"You okay?" he asked, lightly touching my arm.

"Yeah," I said weakly, not sounding at all convincing. I felt like I was about to implode.

He frowned at me. "The fact you're a disturbing shade of

green begs to differ. That place making you physically sick now?"

I laughed. "No, it just so happens that place seems to magnify an already horrific hangover," I informed him.

He gave a knowing grimace. "Yeah, I can imagine that does not do wonders for any kind of ailment... hangovers even more so..." He paused. "Want me to take you for a coffee? Maybe some greasy food?"

I considered it. Yeah, I knew this guy alluded to wanting more, but his suggestion seemed platonic, friendly. He was nice, understood the shit that I was going through. Well, maybe not everything, but stuff pertaining to my grandma and that place. I suspected, with the pain in his eyes that he needed someone to talk to as well. Also, facing a male who wasn't completely and utterly furious with my hungover self-factored in there too.

"Yeah, that sounds good," I agreed finally.

He grinned and his hand went lightly to my lower back. "How about we take my car? I'm worried about the chances of your being able to operate a motor vehicle right now," he joked.

I let him lead me into the parking lot. "Yeah, I might have to agree with you there."

He stopped us in front of a shiny, silver BMW. "Holy shit," I exclaimed. "This is a freaking nice car. Maybe I should become a lawyer. Selling your soul's totally profitable," I commented, my usual lack of filter not hindered by mild alcohol poisoning.

Robert laughed easily and he didn't seem offended by the 'selling your soul' part. He opened the door for me. "Yeah, well, sometimes being a blood sucking lawyer has its perks." He winked at me as I sank into the leather seats.

I laughed easily, genuinely, for the first time since Jim's phone call. It felt good.

"So Macy, apart from subjecting yourself to weekly visits to the asylum. What do you do?" Robert asked, after pulling out of the parking lot.

I glanced over at his attractive profile. "I'm a graphic designer, working from home. I'm a full-time computer hermit, part time *Lord of The Rings* and *Star Wars* enthusiast," I told him.

His eyebrows rose. "You're a graphic designer?" he repeated. "And like *Star Wars*?"

I grinned slightly. "Why, you don't think a computer geek can be someone other than a slightly overweight man living in his mom's basement?" I teased.

He laughed. "No, it's not that, I just haven't encountered one quite as interesting and beautiful as you," he commented.

I blushed. Maybe he wasn't interested in the purely platonic.

"Our firm's actually looking for some new logos, website redesign, I might have to look at your work," he mused, pulling into the parking lot of a trendy looking coffee shop.

And with that, somehow Robert seemed to move my mind out of the dark recesses it had retreated to and made me forget about reality, if only for a while.

COFFEE WITH ROBERT took me on a little trip. Showed me what life would be like if I was the kind of girl who drank fancy, complicated coffee in sleek cafes. If I dated a guy who wore three hundred dollar sweaters and drove fifty thousand dollar cars. It was nice. Comfortable even. But it wasn't me. I knew that. Whatever complications I had with Hansen, whatever shit we had to get through after the last few days, we'd get through it.

So, after a couple of hours on holiday in the *real* world, I hopped in my car and drove back to *my* world. The one where I belonged. At least, where I thought I belonged. One step through the doorway of the place I thought of as home had those thoughts, and my heart, shattering into a thousand pieces.

NINE

I never forget a face. I wasn't shit hot with names, but faces I was good with. This particular face was etched into my brain. Ditto with the name. You don't really forget the guy that shot your parents for apparently seeing something they shouldn't have. You don't forget the man who took away your family and ruined your life.

Seems like he wasn't done taking away my life, my family, because when I walked through the doors to the club, he was sitting in front of the bar smiling and joking with *my family*. He clapped his hand on Hansen's back, laughing at something. He was breathing free air. He was laughing with the men I loved. *Him.* The man who robbed me of everything.

I struggled to breathe as I felt everything collapse around me. My heart seemed to pound so loud it deafened me. My blood boiled and every ounce of anger I'd swallowed over the years burned through my veins.

I didn't register anything. Not Hansen's shocked face as he saw me standing in the doorway, not the way that Grim's level gaze darted from the animal to me. Not Jagger calmly walking up to me, trying to direct me gently out the door. *Nothing*.

All I saw was the gun tucked into Jagger's jeans, visible from the angle he was leaning to get me out the door. Because he was doing that, he didn't expect me to yank the gun out of his belt, calmly switch off the safety and rush to where Hansen was sitting. Everyone seemed to freeze as I lifted the barrel and shot through the face that had been etched into my brain for twelve years.

The gunshot served as something to slow my heart, to regain sound. I felt something warm splatter on my face and then there were arms around me, frenzied curses, a huge amount of not so organized chaos. I didn't really pay attention to it. The anger seeped away as someone yanked the gun out of my hands, and I was half carried by familiar arms to the sofa area. I felt numb. Seeing everything going on around me, but not registering it. My ears rang slightly.

"Holy fuck!" I heard someone yell.

"Make sure no one heard that shit. Get this place locked down and the body out of sight *now*," Grim's calm voice demanded.

Hansen's face dominated my vision and stopped me from focusing on the surrounding commands. His face was concerned, on the edge of panic.

"Macy, look at me," he said calmly, his voice not betraying a thing. His hands grasped the sides of my neck.

I looked at him blankly.

"Talk to me, baby," he pleaded softly.

I stayed silent. I was looking at him, but not really seeing him. It was almost like I was looking through him. I felt like I'd taken a handful of Xanax or smoked an insane amount of weed. Everything was fuzzy.

"Hansen, you need to get Macy the fuck out of here *now*. Levi's with you," a sharp voice ordered.

My eyes moved over to Grim, who was standing watching me with cold eyes. Levi stood behind him, his usually carefree face hard and slightly pale.

Jagger was staring at me off to the side, staring at me like he had no idea who I was.

Charley came up beside Levi. "Holy fuck, I was gonna put my money on any bitch shooting someone in here, it'd be Kim and she'd be shooting off Hammer's dick for not making her his Old Lady," he commented, his eyes wide, observing me.

Levi smacked him upside the head, his face still serious.

Hansen kept his eyes on me, hands firm at my neck.

"Macy," he repeated.

"*Now*, Hansen," Grim ordered.

Hansen didn't look his way but nodded. He clutched my arm and half dragged me toward the back exit. I focused on the pictures on the walls, the ones that I'd thought of as my family portraits. Ones I didn't even recognize anymore. I tried not to think of that, tried not to glance over at the body that was sprawled meters away. The body missing a chunk of head. The body I'd created.

THEY'D TAKEN me to a cabin in the middle of nowhere. A cabin I didn't recognize, and one that had seen better days. The paint was peeling and the air smelled slightly musty. A television was in front of the lumpy sofa I was sitting on, and it was covered in dust.

"What the fuck were you thinking, Macy?" Hansen roared while he paced in front of me.

I flinched at his tone. The gentleness of before was long gone.

There hadn't been talking on the ride here, considering I'd been on the back of Hansen's bike, pressed up against him. When we'd arrived, I'd been unceremoniously dragged in here and deposited on the sofa. Hansen had started pacing. Levi leant on the stained counter. He stepped forward slightly, eyes flickering to me.

"Calm, brother," he muttered, a hand on Hansen's shoulder.

Hansen's shrugged the hand off and moved his furious glare from me to Levi.

"Calm?" he repeated. "Fuck calm! She just fucking shot a man in the middle of the fucking club. Broad daylight! With witnesses!" he yelled. "Lucky it was only patched members in attendance, that's not to say someone wouldn't have heard the shots, maybe called the cops." He started pacing again.

Levi stood in front of him. "No need to worry about that shit, unless there's cause. Lock it down," he ordered.

Hansen nodded stiffly, moved his eyes to me then stormed out of the house, slamming the door behind him.

I flinched again at the noise but stayed silent.

I heard Levi's sigh and his boots made their way over to me. He knelt down so his face was level with mine. His eyes were hard but his expression was gentle.

"You think I'm gonna go to jail?" I asked with a weird sort

of detachment. Nothing had sunk in yet. I had the numbness I had chased last night. And a weird feeling of peace.

Levi squeezed my leg. "Not if we got anythin' to do with it, darlin'," he said softly.

"I don't mind, you know?" I said in that same cold voice. "If I do. I'd rather not if I had a choice, I don't like the outfits and I'm not too keen on being someone's bitch. But I know what I did... broke the law, killed someone..." I shrugged. I knew I should have been feeling something right now. Scared. Disgusted in myself. Guilty. I felt nothing. Only relief.

Levi regarded me. "You're a smart girl, Macy. Shooting someone in the middle of the club... not smart," he said carefully.

"Guess not," I agreed.

There was a pause.

"He killed my parents," I said by way of explanation. "He deserved it."

Levi nodded. This was of no surprise to him. *He knew.* That meant the club knew, and they welcomed him in. Laughed with him. With a murderer. My parents' murderer.

"Club going to make me disappear now?" I asked, chewing over what my actions meant. I may not go to jail, but I'd just broken a pretty big fucking rule. Not only were women never meant to get involved in club business, but I was also pretty sure they weren't meant to murder business associates in the middle of the clubhouse.

Levi's frame jolted. "Make you disappear?" he repeated with disbelief.

I nodded. "You know." I made my finger gun like Arianne had two night previous. I put it to my own head.

Levi clutched the hand with the finger gun and squeezed it

tightly. "Jesus girl," he muttered. "Can't say I know what's gonna happen. Can imagine Grim's not gonna be happy right now, but no one's gonna hurt you. You're family," he said firmly.

I laughed bitterly and snatched my hand out of his grasp. *Family—yeah, right.* I didn't have any of that. Family didn't welcome murderers into the family home. "Yeah, that's what I thought too," I said flatly.

Levi's face hardened and he looked like he was going to say something, but his head jerked to the doorway.

"No one's gonna kill you, Mace. Can't say I'm feeling warm fuzzies toward you at the moment, though. In fact, I'm very tempted to show you the back of my hand," a hard voice declared.

Grim stepped into the room, his face tight. I met his eyes without fear. Most of my emotions seemed to have left the building.

"You wanna tell me what was going through your mind when you decided to walk into my club and shoot a man?" he asked quietly.

I shrugged. "I didn't exactly go in there with that in mind," I said honestly. "But when you walk into a place you consider home and see the man who shot your parents in the face and subsequently ruined your childhood. You feel like returning the favor," I told him blandly.

He stared at me, something working behind his eyes. "You know club rules, Macy? Been around long enough to know them?"

I nodded. "Yeah, I've been around long enough to know them. Long enough to consider the club my everything. My family. I'm happy to respect those rules, backward and sexist as they are. I'm happy to accept the fact that in your world you haven't quite caught on to the fact women have been enjoying equal rights for the past few decades..." I paused. "I don't even care that the club is into some shady shit that comes with the life I've decided to live. I'm happy to overlook all of that, 'cause what I get in return makes it worth it. Or it did..." I narrowed my eyes. "But you welcome a murderer, *my parents' murderer*, knowingly welcome him into your lives? Makes me realize, I've never been part of your family. So how about you shove your rules right up the back of your bike's exhaust," I suggested with venom.

There was a heavy silence once I'd uttered my last word. Levi was regarding me with wide eyes. Hansen had entered the room when I wasn't looking. His face was thunder, and he held himself tautly, eyes on Grim as if he was expecting him to do something. Like he was expecting to have to attack his president in defense of me.

Grim surprised the shit out of everyone in the room by grinning slightly.

"You're lucky it's only Levi and Hansen in here darlin'. Otherwise, I'd be obligated to treat that little performance, and the disrespect, a lot differently." His words may have been easy, but I heard the veiled threat. "As it is, I know both these men care for you a great deal. One arguably more than the other, considering he's claimed you."

My eyes involuntarily locked with Hansen's for a moment. It was coming back in, all of it, the feelings.

"So," Grim continued, oblivious to the moment, "...I'll be chalking that up to the fact that you've had a... *trying* day." He stepped forward. "You're lucky that it just so happens that that scumbag was on our shit list, on account of the fact he robbed someone in our family of their parents, among other things." He paused. "If you don't get the club in serious shit with your impulsive and reckless trigger finger, I'll still consider you part of my family, provided you aren't armed in the future," he added. "The fact the ATF of Feds weren't parked outside our door today, it's just dumb luck." He stepped forward. "You do something like that again, put the club in danger, I won't be so forgiving," he promised.

We held eye contact for a long time and I tried to let his words sink in.

Grim didn't let me say anything, didn't wait for a response. He turned to Levi. "Keep her here, till we can get this shit taken care of," he ordered.

Levi nodded.

He gave me another look then left.

I stood there listening to the sound of a Harley roar off, feeling two sets of eyes on me. I didn't think about that, though. The shock, the adrenaline, it was all wearing off. That wall that separated what I just done from the rest of me falling away.

I killed a man.

On that thought, I darted out of the room and into what I guessed correctly was the bathroom. I made it just in time to empty the meager contents of my stomach. I felt a presence behind me, felt his hands rubbing my back.

I failed to feel embarrassed over the fact he was watching me vomit. He'd just saw me blow a man's head off, it was safe to say he was already disgusted with me. I'd blown myself firmly off that pedestal and into the gutter.

I finally finished emptying my stomach, trying to purge away the feeling that had settled under my skin once I pulled that trigger. I feared that it would never go away. It was burned on my soul forever.

Hansen helped me off the floor and I didn't look at him. I moved to the grimy sink, planning on splashing water in my mouth. That was until I caught a glimpse of my reflection. My blood splattered face. I froze. I knew I couldn't throw up anymore, but I felt the overwhelming urge to empty the poisonous bile at the bottom of my stomach. I slowly looked down to my white tee, it was flecked with splatters of red.

I started shaking. My entire body, so hard I felt my teeth clatter together.

Hansen's hands fastened over mine, he tilted my chin to capture my eyes.

"Breathe, baby, it's okay," he whispered.

"It-it's not okay, I'm co-covered in blood," I stuttered. "I need to get it off, *now*," I said trying to rip my hands from his. I needed to scrub every inch of evidence of what I'd done from my body.

He moved his hands to my neck. "You're going into shock, baby. You need to breathe."

I tried to jerk out of his grasp, he held me tight. "I need to get it off!" I screeched hysterically.

Hansen seemed to get it, he nodded and released my hands. Moving to close the door, I heard him turning on a shower. I was too busy ripping my clothes off, needing them away, somewhere where I couldn't see them, couldn't feel them.

Hansen moved back to me, silently taking over undressing me. Once I was naked, I stood there shivering, not from the cold in the air that prickled my bare skin, but from the inside that chilled my veins.

Hansen quickly took his own clothes off, mingling them with mine. I didn't have time to question him as he directed us both to the shower. I stood woodenly under the spray, my desperation to get clean seemed to have disappeared. I had turned into some sort of zombie, unable to move, flashbacks what I had done replaying in my brain.

Hansen's hands worked over me, lathering soap into my body, cleaning the outside. I let him, staring into space, only seeing my hand on the trigger. His face exploding.

I barely noticed when he turned off the water, wrapped me in a towel. Lifting me like a baby, he walked us into a sparse bedroom. He set me down and pulled a tee over my head, yanked some jeans on, and placed me carefully on the bed, wrapping me in his arms.

I snuggled into his body, trying to get as close as I could, trying to think of only that, focus on nothing else while my mind shut down.

BLOOD. I jerked awake, sitting up quickly and inspecting my hands with panic, expecting them to be drenched in blood. From the dim light in the room, I saw they were clean. On the outside anyway.

"We good?" I heard a tight voice ask from beyond the closed door.

I moved my head to see the rumpled space beside me. The rumpled empty space.

"Yeah, we're good. No one heard the shot. Got the body taken care of quickly. Clubhouse is clean," a voice clipped.

"Thank fuck." Hansen's relief was evident, even through a wooden door.

"Yeah. That shit could have gone a whole other way. Pure fuckin' luck it worked out the way it did. Your woman endangered the club," the voice was cold. I recognized it as Grim's.

"She was fuckin' faced with the man who ruined her life. What the fuck did you expect? Told you it was a bad idea to bring him anywhere near the club," Hansen's voice was full of anger, but it was quiet like he was trying not to wake the sleeping murderer in the next room.

There was a pause. "I didn't expect her to come in at that particular moment. And I sure as shit didn't expect her reaction to put a bullet in his brain, calm as anything," the voice said dryly. "Fuck, despite myself, I find myself impressed by the bitch's boldness. Maybe not her timing, nor her forethought. But any other female in that situation, most likely turn into a sniveling mess or run. Your woman turns straight to vengeance. Born to be an Old Lady. Ruthless one at that. Better make sure your cock doesn't stray."

I jerked at the words.

"Yeah, don't think anyone thought fuckin' Macy would be the one pulling the trigger on that scumbag," Levi's voice interjected. "I agree, might not have been the best timing, but the girl deserved her revenge. Fuckin' proud she was strong enough to deal it out."

There was silence. Hansen didn't voice any pride or praise at the fact that I'd ended someone's life.

"You stay here for tonight, just so we make sure this shit can't lead back to us. Then bring Macy back to the club, make sure your fuckin' gun's out of reach," Grim added with something close to humor.

I lay there as they all murmured goodbyes. I stared at the ceiling, not knowing what to do with myself. How to even begin the process what I'd heard. The fact all the guilt and sickness I felt seemed to have disappeared. Instead, I felt a weight had been lifted.

The door creaked open and Hansen silently closed it. I felt the bed depress as he moved to lay down and gather me in his arms. I knew he knew I was awake, but I didn't speak for a second.

"So I'm not going to be arrested for murder?" I deduced, my tone flat.

The arms around me tightened. "No babe," he promised. "Club's taken care of it. You won't be going anywhere."

"Remind me to send them a thank you card. Box of choco-lates. Or a case of Jack Daniels," I muttered.

Hansen said nothing.

"That something the club's done before? Clean up bodies?" I asked.

"Once or twice," Hansen told me, to my surprise.

Even that vague answer was more than a woman normally got. Then again, he probably didn't think of me as his woman anymore.

"Do you think I'm disgusting?" I whispered, my voice breaking.

Hansen flipped me, covering my body completely. "Why the fuck would you say something like that?"

"Because I killed someone," I whispered. "Shot someone. Right in front of you. I'm sure murderess isn't something you want your Old Lady to be. You've already got reformed whore on the list."

Hansen jerked. He reached to turn on a lamp beside us. I squinted until I got used to the light.

"Look at me," he commanded.

I did as he ordered, expecting to see hardness, detachment in his eyes. Instead, his face was soft, his eyes looked at me the very same way they did that morning when he made me breakfast. When he changed my world.

"You promised not to use that fuckin' word in reference to yourself again. I'm tempted to put you over my knee right now, but I'll delay." His eyes searched mine, swimming the depths of my soul. "Nothing will ever make me think of you as anything less than you are," he promised. "And what you are, is magnificent."

"But I shot someone," I argued. "Right in the head." My body jolted at the memory.

Hansen's face didn't waver. His hand gently traced my lips. "Yeah, babe. You shot the piece of shit who tried to rob you of everything good in your life. Who took two loving parents away from a little girl. The man who didn't succeed, thank fuck, in taking away your light, your goodness."

He paused. "You exacted revenge. You gave him what he deserved. And trust me, baby, he deserved to eat that bullet." His brows furrowed. "Did I want you to have to be the one to deliver it? No. I meant what I said when I wanted to protect you from everything I could. I'm fuckin' in awe you found it in yourself to bring him to justice. But I didn't want you to have to do it. Wasn't too keen on the time and place either," he added with a small twinkle in his eye.

I stilled. Everything he said was something I could have wished for.

"So you don't hate me?" I asked in a small voice.

"Jesus, babe, I could never hate you. Not when I love you more than anything in this world. Not when you own my heart," he said firmly.

I sagged. Then I pounced. I pushed at his chest and managed to roll him, so I was straddling him. I didn't waste any time, I attached my mouth to his, kissing him with a brutality I didn't even know I was capable of.

All I knew was I needed him, and I had to have him inside me in that moment. It had to be rough and hard and all consuming.

The way his hands yanked off the tee I was wearing while he rolled me back onto my back and cocked my leg roughly to circle his hip, I knew he needed it too. His other hand tightly encircled my neck, not to the point of pain, but enough to make me feel, make my only thoughts be of him and his body.

"Need you inside me, *now,*" I demanded hoarsely, my mouth inches from his.

"Gonna eat your pussy first," he growled, kissing me firmly before working his way down.

I cried out as his mouth fastened on my clit after paying close attention to my nipples. I was already ready to climax as he devoured me like a starving man. It was relentless, nowhere near the gentle, teasing way his mouth normally worked me. So, when I exploded it was a reflection of the brutal way he brought me to climax. I couldn't even hold in my scream, especially not when his body settled over mine and plunged into me, hard, rough, and beautiful. His thrusts pounded against my tender flesh, causing the tension to build right as it had just settled. I could barely breathe as his mouth took control of mine, plundering it while he pounded into me, the taste if my arousal on his lips.

"You'll always be mine," he promised against my mouth. "Always, no matter what."

His words were enough to send me over the edge once more, enough to take me past the brink of coherent thought. My mind only on the pleasure.

Hansen's whole body turned taut and he buried his face in my neck, latching his teeth and marking me as he came.

When we were done, we were both sticky with sweat from our frenzied lovemaking, both breathing hard. Hansen hovered above me, watching me. He kissed my nose gently.

"I'll always love you, babe, no matter what," he said quietly.

Maybe it was the post orgasm glow or the resolution in those words, but something made me believe him. Made me think that despite the mess I was in, everything was going to be okay.

"SOMETHING GRIM SAID BEFORE, got me thinking," I murmured, tucked up against Hansen's chest.

It was late. After we'd made love, Hansen had left to get us some food, which we ate in bed. He then made love to me again, this time slower, gentler, but no less mind-blowing. We had lain in silence a long while, until now.

"Yeah, babe, what's that?"

"You were already planning on killing him?" I didn't say his name. I never would. I'd heard somewhere that someone died two deaths. Their actual physical death, when they took their last breath, and another kind of death, when everyone in the world stopped saying their name. I had taken care of the first death, I was hell bent on taking care of the second as well.

I felt the chest below me tighten. "Yeah, we were," he admitted.

I moved my head up to meet his eyes. "Why?" I whispered.

Hansen's face turned hard. "Arianne called me not long after I left you yesterday," he started.

I flinched thinking of the way that day had started. What he'd told me about his mother. I could only focus on one thing at a time, though. So I listened.

"She was worried you might have succumbed to alcohol poisoning, her words not mine." He grinned slightly. "So she told me why you decided to disappear into a vodka bottle," his voice lost all amusement. "Soon as I found out, I knew I'd be making sure that fucker didn't breathe free for long, not after what he did. Told the boys, they were happy to assist." He searched my face. "Fate has a fuckin' warped sense of humor, babe."

I furrowed my brows, not understanding.

"Stephen Ross was a patched member of the Sons of Templar, New Mexico charter, just over fourteen years ago," he told me.

My entire body froze. "No," I whispered.

"Yeah babe, he was a member. That was until he tried to get himself rich while he double crossed the club. Betrayed his brothers." His voice was sharp. "I wasn't a member then, babe, but Grim and Levi were. So they remember the blow that was. Blow they couldn't return when he found himself for murdering a couple in their own home." He watched my face as the blood drained from it. "Grim's been waiting for the fucker to get out of prison, to exact revenge with his own two hands," he carried on. "When he got word the fucker got paroled, he reached out, pretended that the past was buried. Of course, just before Ross rolled into the club, we learned his connection to you. What he did. That knowledge had Ross's fate become infinitely darker. A lot more bloody."

I gaped at him. "This is too freaky to believe," I said finally.

Hansen's arms tightened. "Yeah babe, the universe works in fucked up ways sometimes. In the end, Ross got what he deserved. Club got the revenge it craved, even if it was at the hands of a pixie-haired half pint who radiated light and goodness," he said softly.

TEN

One Month Later

I stared at the screen. I'd been staring at it for five hours straight and my eyes hurt. My back ached. But my mind was busy. That was good. Necessary. My mind needed to be occupied, it could never be empty. With emptiness came memories.

The past month I'd battled against them. Against the dreams that jerked me awake at night. The flashbacks that had me lose my breakfast. It was hard. I'd killed a man. Yes, he was evil, the worst kind, but it didn't change what I'd done. And what I'd done had changed me. I tried to keep my optimism, my happy outlook, my smile. I buried myself in work, baked up a freaking storm in Hansen's kitchen, went out with Arianne when Hansen had to be at the club. Though, I never had more than a couple of drinks, mindful of the demons that Hansen had buried. Of the mother he was yet to talk about. That might be because he was too busy watching me with an eagle eye, waiting for me to have my inevitable breakdown.

The first time I went to the club was the hardest. Saw the spot where I'd done it. The spot which had obviously been scrubbed clean, losing any evidence that it was the location of a murder. I had expected the men to be mad, furious at the fact that I had endangered the club, put them all at risk, made them dispose of a body for me. I'd been beyond surprised at the nods of respect, at the gentle squeezes they gave me, devoid of any form of anger. The biggest surprise was Hammer. He had approached me after Jagger had kissed my cheek with a sad glint to his vibrant emerald eyes. Hansen turned to stone beside me, mindful of the fact Hammer didn't exactly love women. Hammer ignored him.

"Took guts... what you did. Was stupid as fuck, don't get me wrong, and had you done anything to make the club go down for it, I wouldn't be standing in front of you right now," he started roughly.

Hansen made a sound in his throat and stepped forward, I pulled on his hand, stopping him.

"But, club's good. So that's a non-issue. Get the need for revenge, for justice, didn't think a bitch like you would have the stomach to carry it out," he continued as if Hansen hadn't almost just charged him. He didn't say anything else, merely nodded to me and walked off.

I'd been utterly shocked at that speech. One that hinted there was more to Hammer than an apparent resentment of women and temper problems. Something that caused those eyes to turn dark and empty.

That was the last the guys spoke of it. Everyone treated me as normal, apart from Jagger, who was a bit softer with me than usual, like he was expecting me to fall apart. Hansen was the same, he had spent every spare second with me. He tried to act normal, but every now and then I saw concern seep into his features.

He was the only reason I made it through. I couldn't tell Arianne. Obviously, I couldn't tell anyone apart from the handful of men who already witnessed it. So Hansen was the one who gave me strength, who held me tight when nightmares jerked me awake. Who made love to me like I was still his everything, despite my actions. I was slowly coming back to myself, with the support of my family, my man, my club. But that didn't mean I didn't have a long way to go.

I tried my best to keep to my routine, including visiting Grandma, which didn't do much for my state of mind. Robert and I had weekly coffee dates after our respective visits. I found it refreshing, talking to someone completely removed from my lifestyle. Someone who didn't know I was a murderer.

"Babe?" Hansen's voice jerked me out of the past and into the present.

I moved my head from the computer screen to fasten my eyes to his. They were brimming with concern. "How long you been sitting in front of that thing?" he asked tightly.

I stood and stretched. "Ummm... depends on how long you think I've been sitting there," I hedged.

Hansen's hungry eyes roved over my denim cut-offs and white tee that read, *'I'm not short, I'm a hobbit.'* His mouth turned into a grin and he shook his head, tagging my waist so my body collided with his.

"How many of those things do you have?" he murmured against my mouth.

"I haven't got an exact number, but it's in double digits," I informed him.

He chuckled.

"Never thought I'd find that geek shit as hot as I do, babe. But somehow it manages to get my cock hard as stone," he said, his whiskers tickling my cheek.

I smiled at him. "Well sir, we may just have to do something about that," I informed him in a throaty voice.

I kissed him what I intended to be lightly, but instead he clutched the back of my head and beautifully claimed my mouth. I almost forgot my mission once he'd released me, but the hard on pressing against my stomach reminded me. I winked my slightly dreamy eye, moving down his body, lovingly running my hands along his cut.

When I knelt to the floor and released him from his jeans, I licked my lips, moving forward to taste the pre-cum at the head of his cock.

He hissed and his hands went to lightly cradle my head. I took him fully into my mouth, loving the whispered curse of pleasure he emitted. I worked him lovingly, running my hands along his shaft as I sucked, moving slow but deep.

"Macy," he grunted, his voice rough with desire.

I kept going.

"Macy," he repeated. "Gonna cum, babe. You don't want me to fill up that sweet mouth, you stop now," he ordered.

I inwardly grinned, arousal building up in my stomach as I worked him harder and warm liquid shot into my mouth as Hansen's hands tightened on my head.

"Fuck," he half shouted.

I slowly licked him clean, and then his arms went under my armpits to lift me.

"Jesus, baby," he murmured, lifting me.

I grinned at him.

He started us toward his bedroom. "Gonna eat you till you

scream, Macy. Then I'll fuck you till you forget your own name," he growled, throwing me on the bed.

And for the next two hours, he kept his promise.

IT WAS SATURDAY. For some, Saturday signaled the start of a blissful, relaxing weekend. For me, it was the opposite. Even though I'd pulled up to the house of dread plastered to Hansen's back, I couldn't escape the swirling in my stomach knowing I'd have to spend an hour with her.

"Don't like you going in there, babe. Don't like that your eyes don't get their light back until at least a couple of hours after you leave her," Hansen said after I'd reluctantly peeled myself off his bike.

I smiled at him. "You're just going to have to make sure you get creative in finding ways to make my eyes bright again." I winked, trying to keep my cheery façade strong. Maybe if I acted it, I'd feel it.

His eyes turned dark. "You fuckin' bet I will, babe.'

My stomach dropped at the erotic promise. I smacked his shoulder. "You can't get me all aroused before I go into the real life version of *Night of the Living Dead*," I scolded him.

He smirked. "Way I see it, the only way you'll get through that is if you're thinking of my dick. Pick you up in an hour?"

I shook my head, feeling turned on despite myself. "I'm having coffee with a friend after. So pick me up from that fancy coffee place on Wilson Street in two hours, if that's okay? Otherwise, I can get a cab," I added.

Hansen's face hardened. "You're not getting a cab. I'll be there. Now give me your mouth," he instructed.

I bent down, as he was still sitting on his bike. He tagged the back of my neck and laid one on me, hot and heavy, in the middle of the parking lot.

Once he'd released me, I stood back with a dreamy look on my face.

"That's a promise of what's to come," he murmured.

"That will definitely get me through *The Night of the Living Dead*," I said dreamily.

His eyes softened. "Love you, babe."

My stomach dropped like it did every time he said that. "Love you, too," I half whispered.

He gave me one more look then took off, leaving me standing there watching his bike drive away. I took a deep breath and faced the building.

———

I SURVIVED THE VISIT, with only minor internal damage from the sharp points of Grandma's words. It helped I had some complicated and delicious coffee smothered in cream afterward. I was also distracted by seemingly insignificant problems when Robert opened up to me over said coffee. My heart had broken for him, yet he stayed reasonably strong until we walked outside onto the street, saying our goodbyes.

"I'm so sorry, Bob," I told him sincerely. Since we'd become friends, I took to calling Robert, Bob. Mostly because no one called him that, and he smirked every time I did it. He was so not a Bob.

He squeezed me before letting me go. "Thanks, Macy," he said, his eyes watering slightly.

Bob had told me his mother was completely gone, even the

fleeting glimpses he used to get off her were snatched from the cruel disease holding her mind hostage.

"Call me if you want to talk?" I said, worried about the fact he didn't seem to have any friends he spoke of, any other family to talk to. He was a nice guy, he deserved someone.

He gave me a sad smile. "Will do, Mace. This would've been a lot harder had I not had you to help me through." He kissed me on the head lightly then turned to the parking lot.

I stood watching him for a second, then turned back to the street, about to get my phone to call Hansen. I didn't expect to see him sitting on his bike, directly across the street. He did not look happy.

"Hey honey, sorry, I hope you haven't been waiting long," I said after I made it to his bike, my body relaxing in his presence.

"Who the fuck was that?" he said in greeting, his eyes on the BMW pulling out of the parking lot.

"That's my friend, Bob," I said carefully, noting the anger in his voice.

He moved his eyes back to me. "You didn't think of telling me about your friend... Bob?" he muttered.

I put my hands on my hips. "Is this because I didn't tell you, or because Bob happens to have a penis?" I asked snippily. "I'm allowed to have male friends, Hansen."

His jaw clenched. "Yeah babe, not too keen on you hiding them from me. Nor am I too keen on the fact he wants a taste of your pussy."

Something in his words, the crassness of them maybe, or maybe it was because I was coasting on frazzled emotions, but something made me lose it.

"You think I'm going to give it to him?" I hissed. "You think once a whore always a whore?"

Hansen actually flinched and his face turned hard. "Told you not to call yourself that, Macy," he growled, moving to get off his bike.

I scuttled back onto the sidewalk. "Why not?" I yelled. "That's what I was. What I always will be. It's never going to change. You think 'cause I've been with everyone in the club, I'll let any man who buys me an expensive latte have a piece of me?"

Hansen stalked forward. "Jesus, Macy, calm down. That's not what I fuckin' said," he thundered, his face tight.

I threw my hands out, not caring we were having this out in the middle of the street. "It's what you were thinking. I was a fool to think I could do this, be with you, transition into an Old Lady when you saw me as a club whore," I spat, my chest heaving.

I didn't know where this was coming from, this anger. I knew it was that little seed I'd nurtured through the start of our relationship, maturing, growing too big to hide anymore or to run from. I was already running from the events of a month ago. It had all finally caught me.

Hansen's face turned thunderous and he stepped forward again, clutching my hips tightly.

"I've never thought of you like that. Not once. 'Cause you never fuckin' were. You're special. Not one in a million, once in a lifetime. You are more than any label can describe, especially that fuckin' ugly one you keep spewing out," he growled, though his eyes were soft. "You're a woman who's stronger than any man I've met. Whose smile lights up a room. You can make the hardest men I know laugh just by babbling some bullshit about fairies and wizards. Just by being you. You. Macy... my Old Lady. That's the only label you have, the only one I care about," he told me firmly, holding my eyes hostage.

Tears streamed down my face. I couldn't hold it together any longer. Everything I'd been burying inside bubbled out through my tear ducts, my body starting to shake with my sobs.

Hansen wiped them away, all trace of anger gone from his beautiful face. "Shit," he muttered. His hand cupped my jaw. "Look at me," he commanded.

I met his piercing blue eyes, my vision slightly blurry.

"You're gonna get on the back of my bike where you belong. Where you'll always belong, then we'll go home," he declared firmly.

"Ca-can we watch *Lord of the Rings*?" I hiccupped, needing my fantasy world now more than ever.

Hansen shook his head, a shadow of a smile on his face. "Yeah babe," he kissed my nose. "On the bike," he whispered.

I looked at him a moment, then moved to sit on the back of his beautiful Harley, where I belonged.

"YOU LOVED IT, ADMIT IT," I said, once the credits on *Fellowship of The Ring* started rolling.

Hansen moved me so I was completely on top of him on the sofa.

"Love that it put a smile on my girl's beautiful face. Put the light back in her eyes. Would watch that every day for the rest of my life if that's what it takes," he told me, his eyes intent on me. "Want to talk about it, babe? What that shit was before?"

I looked down, my hands fiddling with the fabric on his

tee. I didn't know if I did want to talk about what made me effectively have a breakdown in the middle of the street, but I knew I needed to. Otherwise, all that crap would fester, come back up again, and poison me with its negativity. I'd been bottling it up for a month, over a month, ever since Hammer's words hit home that night at the club.

Hansen's hand went to my chin. "Look at me, baby," he said softly.

I swallowed, looking into his eyes. "I'm just waiting for it to happen," I whispered softly.

His brows furrowed. "What?"

"Something... something awful. Something that shatters all of this," I explained my worst fear. "I've never been happier in my life when I'm with you. On the bike, off your bike," I said, and his arms tightened around me. "I'm not used to loving someone this much. To having everything I've always dreamed of. He came and took it away when he ended my parents' lives. Then he came back, and I'm still haunted by him. Still terrified one day you're going to realize you don't want to share your life with a reformed club girl and murderer," I said in a small voice. "I can live with my title as former club girl. I don't regret it, not for a second. It gave me family, gave me you. The murderer one? Not so much."

Hansen flipped us, in one fluid movement, and he was quickly on top of me. "Lot a shit wrong with what you just said, baby," he started in a hard tone. "Lot that makes my fuckin' heart break, knowing that it's been stewing in that beautiful head of yours for a long time," he stroked my head. "Knew that shit a month ago would haunt you. Your soul is good, down to the core, not an ounce of black in it." He looked at me, his eyes searching mine. "You're not a fuckin' murderer.

You're a survivor, a fuckin' miracle, one I thank God or whoever's controlling the strings up there for," he said firmly. "Your past with the club? It's never gonna get to me, babe. Get that through your head. I love you. Every inch of you. I'll never resent you, or think of you differently 'cause you were a club girl." He stroked my face. "'Cause if you weren't, I'd never would've met you. Something that doesn't even bear thinking of... a life without you in it. I'll love you till the moment the reaper claims me, even after that, too. I plan on planting a baby in you, making a family with you, forever," he declared. "I'll do whatever it takes, remind you every day of what a fuckin' magnificent creature you are, to make sure you don't ever think ugly thoughts about yourself again."

I sucked in a breath. Everything he said made my heart pound, made it feel like it might explode. A baby? It should have freaked me out. I was too young. I was recovering from shooting my parents' killer in front of my old man and his brothers, but yet, the thought calmed me. Made me smile on the inside. No, beam on the inside.

I had it. Family. Forever.

EPILOGUE

One Year Later

"Breathe," I whispered to my reflection.

I sucked in a huge breath, trying to use the air as an instrument to quell the butterflies fluttering in my stomach.

"You can do this," I told my reflection again. My reflection, that didn't even look like me. Well, I guess it did. My pixie cut had grown out a bit but I had kept it short and choppy. Most of the time it was artfully mussed in the 'I just got out of bed look,' mostly because I didn't do it when I got out of bed. Lately, my thoughts were not of taming my hair. I was mostly skipping around the house in a post orgasmic glow. Hansen was a firm believer in morning sex and it was safe to say I was a convert.

But now, my usually messed hair was curled into soft curls while a daisy crown graced my head, in my true flower child style. My makeup was subtle though I was wearing false eyelashes because a girl always needed a hint of glam. It was the dress that did it. The pure white, long sleeved, vintage lace gown and it was the most beautiful thing I'd ever seen. The v-neck hinted at cleavage while still being demure, the soft lace hugged my body until it met my waist, tulle replacing the lace and flowing down in a soft waterfall. It was almost completely backless. It was my dream dress. I was getting married to my dream man. The past year had been a blissful fantasy. It wasn't easy, nor was the relationship with the love of my life always smooth sailing. But it was real. Magical. Not the kind with elves and wizards, but the real life kind, the stuff I didn't even know existed.

That's why my hands were shaking. Why the butterflies were churning in my stomach. You woke up from dreams. They ended and reality came seeping back. I was terrified one person couldn't be this happy. That happiness wouldn't always follow me wherever I went, that real life would catch up and shatter it all.

"Holy fuck," I heard a masculine voice mutter from the doorway.

I whirled around and my breath left me. Hansen was standing across the room from me, in black slacks, a white shirt and his cut over the top. A single daisy poked out from the pocket. He was drool worthy.

"Didn't think you'd get any more beautiful to me, babe," he whispered, stalking toward me. "But now I know beauty is not a word that can be used to describe how you look... how you radiate. Word hasn't even been invented yet," he murmured, making it over to me. His eyes never left mine, his hands spanned my waist.

"You're not supposed to see the bride before the wedding, it's bad luck," I protested vainly, my eyes locked in his stare.

My heart nearly exploding in the love in his gaze, the reverence. His eyes were softening, opening up for me and me only. The devotion in them was something I'd woken up to every day for a year. The thing I'd dreamed of when I first set foot in the club.

The hands at my waist tightened. "Think we've both had our share of bad luck, Macy," he said against my mouth. "My luck changed the moment I set foot into the club..." his finger trailed against my jaw, "...hit the fuckin' jackpot the moment I tasted those lips in the middle of the night a year later."

He pushed me back, so I hit the table in the room that was designated as my dressing room in the big lodge in the middle of nowhere, where we were getting married. Before I knew it, he had lifted me, gently pulling my dress up.

"Wha-what are you doing?" I whispered, my breath catching as his finger pushed passed my panties.

Ice blue eyes met mine. "Gonna fuck you, baby," he told me, his eyes flaring.

I let out a little squeak as his finger pushed into me. "But we're about to get married," I protested weakly.

"Yeah babe and this memory is going down as the best day of my life. Wanna be standing up there, tying myself to you forever, knowing the flush on your face is from me fuckin' you senseless," he half growled, pushing his pants down and positioning himself at my entrance.

No way in hell I could argue with that.

He paused, one hand on my neck. "This ain't ever gonna go bad, Mace. This... us... it's always gonna be solid. I'm always gonna love you with every inch of my soul. Nothing will change that," he promised fiercely.

"I love you, too, forever," I whispered back, with tears in my eyes.

He plunged into me the same moment his lips met mine, his mouth gentle against mine while he pounded into me.

"Gonna plant our child inside you, babe," he grunted, lifting his mouth from mine.

I was deep in a sex haze, already transfixed by his previous words, I barely registered the statement. All I knew was the orgasm I was chasing was set to shatter my world. Somewhere deep inside, a warm glow settled at the image of having a family with Hansen, growing his child inside me. Right now, I couldn't focus on that.

Hansen kept going, clutching my collarbone as he pressed his nose against mine, his eyes holding me captive. I cried out as my orgasm hit me unexpectedly, fireworks exploding through my body, I clutched onto Hansen as I rode the wave. I felt his body tighten at his own release and he pressed his lips against mine.

We stayed locked together, connected, while we both caught our bearings, breathing heavily.

Hansen kissed my head tenderly before he slowly pulled out of me. I stayed where I was, slightly dazed. I was thinking about the unfortunate logistics of getting married straight after having unprotected sex when Hansen returned with a hot washcloth.

He lovingly, and slowly cleaned himself from me and I watched his head.

"Did you mean that?" I said finally.

He looked up, a small smile on his face. "What babe?"

I paused. "The baby thing," I said in a small voice.

Why I was nervous, I had no idea, I was marrying the man

for Christ's sake, babies were an obvious conclusion. But I was still young, and Hansen was still away a lot with club business. Kids weren't something that I'd even thought of. Okay, I'd thought of them. Any girl in love with a man like Hansen would think about what he would look like cradling a baby.

Hot is the answer.

He paused and tossed the washcloth aside. His hands went to my neck.

"I've never been more serious about anything in my life, apart from my feelings for you. Want my ring on your finger, you on the back of my bike, and my baby in your belly," he declared roughly, his eyes sparkling.

My breath left me. I was speechless. Happiness, pure unadulterated happiness didn't need words.

Hansen smiled. "Want to go get married now?" he asked.

I smiled back and nodded.

Twenty minutes later, I was Mrs. Hansen Armstrong.

Nine months later, Xander Armstrong came into the world.

Pure unadulterated happiness followed me wherever I went.

OUT OF THE ASHES

Living a life in darkness causes the soul to char to ash. Battling demons by turning himself into a monster is the only way he can survive...the only way he can keep a grip on sanity. That grip is precarious at best, every day is a silent battle with demons that threaten to yank him into the truest form of darkness, the abyss he'll never escape. Then it happens. Light shines through the cracks.

Happiness. Mia Spencer's life is full of it. She has an amazing new job, friends, family, and the light of her life - her daughter Lexie. Running from the demons of the past, escaping a hell that she vowed Lexie would never know about, she worked through hardship and near poverty to create something she was proud of. Buried deep inside, underneath the swell of love she had for her only daughter, were the fractured pieces of her. Pieces that were smashed and battered when she was young and vulnerable.

Then she meets Bull, who seems to hate her on sight. He screams danger, from his huge physique to his beautiful ink, to the motorcycle club he belongs to. He is silent, his glares threaten to burn her into flames, yet she finds herself falling for him. Finds this broken man slowly fixing the pieces she thought would stay shattered forever.

ABOUT THE AUTHOR

ANNE MALCOM has been an avid reader since before she can remember, her mother responsible for her love of reading. It started with magical journeys into the world of Hogwarts and Middle Earth, then as she grew up her reading tastes grew with her. Her love of reading doesn't discriminate, she reads across many genres, although classics like Little Women and Gone with the Wind will hold special places in her heart. She also can't get enough romance, especially when some possessive alpha males throw their weight around.

One day, in a reading slump, Cade and Gwen's story came to her and started taking up space in her head until she put their story into words. Now that she has started, it doesn't look like she's going to stop anytime soon, with many more characters demanding their story be told as well.

Raised in small town New Zealand, Anne had a truly special childhood, growing up in one of the most beautiful countries in the world. She has backpacked across Europe, ridden camels in the Sahara and eaten her way through Italy, loving every moment. For now, she's back at home in New Zealand and quite happy. But who knows when the travel bug will bite her again.

Want to get in touch with Anne? She loves to hear from her readers.
You can email her: annemalcomauthor@hotmail.com
Or join her reader group on Facebook.

ALSO BY ANNE MALCOLM

The Sons of Templar Series

Making the Cut

Firestorm

Out of the Ashes

Beyond the Horizon

Dauntless

Battles of the Broken

Deadline to Damnation

Scars of Yesterday

Three Kinds of Trouble

The Unquiet Mind Series

Echoes of Silence

Skeletons of Us

Broken Shelves

Mistake's Melody

Censored Soul

Retired Sinners

Splinters of You

Printed in Great Britain
by Amazon

83720459R00082